COLLEGE GUYS RUIN

LIVES

Watch Out! These Guys
Are Not Who You Think They Are!

COLLEGE GUYS RUIN LIVES

Copyright © 2025. All rights reserved.

Table of Contents

Chapter One:
ON MY WAY OUT

Mustard and ketchup stain my apron as I help the next customer in line narrow down what they want to eat. The new guy on sandwiches just got off a smoke break and is having a hard time remembering the order of condiments on the big bacon sandwich: mayo, ketchup, bacon, and cheese.

"Can I also get two 20-piece nuggets?" the customer demands with a slight attitude.

"Yes!" I say with fake enthusiasm.

I look at the nugget tray, where only five nuggets are ready. The other employees are goofing off in the back. The manager on shift is outside with the remaining male employees, smoking weed and talking about the girls they've slept with in the kitchen.

"Huh! It's going to be one of those days," I whisper to myself as I tell the customer it will be a four-minute wait.

Her attitude is now in full effect, but I ignore it and go over to the fryer and drop a bag of nuggets.

The smell of grease is thick, and I have to squint my eyes through my glasses just to see. Glancing at the front door, I see a group of 10 come in, and none of them are the people who work here. The new guy on sandwiches is finally off his phone and is done making the sandwich, only to find out that he will be making six more.

I hear him grunt around the corner where he is stationed.

"Hey! It's almost 5 p.m. The night shift should be on the way in," I tell him.

The sky is somewhat dark when my manager tells me to clock out. I take off my dirty apron and reach up to the crown of my head to pull out the coils in my big puff that sits above my visor cap. The new guy on sandwiches catches my eye and is on his way over.

"Man, that shit was crazy! I don't know if this is for me," he says.

"It's not that bad. You just have to get used to it," I reply.

"You smoke?" he asks.

"Nah, I'm good," I say.

"Damn, you don't smoke? So you cute, and you don't smoke," he says surprisingly.

"I guess so!" I say with a slight smile.

He takes out a blunt and motions me towards the door.

"If you take the bus, I can walk you to the stop. I walk that way, too," he offers.

I usually walk by myself, which is not good, considering the neighborhood has a reputation for robberies, homicides, and police brutality. This is the typical life in St. Louis, Missouri. Without hesitation, I take him up on his offer. The grass in the area hasn't been cut in about two weeks, and trash is thrown everywhere you can think of. The new guy looks at me with glossy dark eyes and a smirk.

"So, who are you? Like, what you got going on?" he asks while he begins to light his blunt.

"Well, I'm going to college in a couple more weeks—the big one, which is a couple of hours away," I respond.

"For real? So you smart and shit? Damn, a smart and cute one. Why you want to go to college, though?"

Is this dude serious? Why wouldn't I want to get away from this neighborhood? I've lived here my entire life, and all I've witnessed were shootings, getting confronted by gang members, girls not liking me because of boys, boys liking me—and over-sexualizing me. Fighting is a universal code in this neighborhood that everyone does. If you hate somebody, you fight; if you like somebody, you fight; if you want to have fun, you fight. I've had to fight dudes several times because they've called me out of my name and they wanted to jump my brother. There's no way I'd watch while my brother is getting jumped.

"Are you crazy?" I say. "This place is too dramatic, and I need to get away. What about you, since you asking all these questions?"

"Look around you and tell me what you see," he says.

I stare around and see burnt-down buildings, police patrolling on almost every corner, a bunch of beauty supplies, fast-food chains, and liquor stores. I can also see men everywhere on each corner, in each store, and on each block.

"The neighborhood?" I respond.

"You see dudes like me who sell drugs, trying to provide for their families," he informs me.

Even though I could have guessed, I can't believe he just told me this about himself.

"You sell drugs?" I ask with surprise.

He takes a puff of his blunt and stares me dead in my eyes.

"Yes. I'm a drug dealer. I sell drugs," he affirms.

"Oh, cool," I respond.

That was awkward as hell. I'm starting to feel weird about the entire conversation. I don't understand why he was comfortable telling me that, but maybe everyone already knows, and I'm behind on street talk. Luckily, my bus is approaching the stop that we had just walked across the intersection to catch. The new guy blinks and nods, and I nod back to let him know I'm good to go.

"See you tomorrow, college girl," he says as he walks away, smoking his nearly gone blunt.

I take the bus for about 15 minutes to the main street, where I have to walk 25 minutes down the street to where my house sits. I can't call anyone to come pick me up because everyone is at work or at home asleep, and they don't want to be bothered. Staring down at my journey, I take a deep breath and start walking.

A luxury black car with tinted windows pulls up and stops on the road beside me. My heart starts to panic, and I feel a shock run down my spine. All I see are bright headlights beaming into the night. I stay frozen in place as the driver rolls the window down slowly. A slender man who looks to be in his mid-20s with locs and tattoos on his forearm stares at me.

"Hey, I see you just getting off the bus stop. You need a ride home?" he says.

I stare at him, then down the road. My body is still stuck in place.

"Um, it's okay. I'm good, but thank you," I say, finally unfreezing and beginning to walk.

The man begins driving to the pace of my walk.

"Look, it's cold and dark, and you probably have a long walk ahead. Let me help you out," he offers.

My eyes turn wide. My lips curl up. I hear a faint voice in my head that says, 'RUN!'

Without hesitation, I sprint down the street with all my might. I begin panting frantically, wishing there was someone I could call to save me. I run a few blocks, and when I no longer see the man's car, I stop. Breathing heavily, I bend down and rest my arms on my legs, gasping for air. I look out into the distance and see the man's car waiting a few feet ahead. My eyes begin searching for the street I'm on, and I realize I still have about 10 more minutes before I reach my house.

There seem to be no other cars on the street right now besides him. He puts his car in reverse and pulls up to my side again.

"Why you running like I'm going to kidnap you or something?" he asks me, then says, "Look, I'm a businessman, and I make a lot of money. I'm not trying to do anything to you. I'm just looking out for you. Come on now. Get in the car."

I feel perplexed by my situation. My mom always said to never get in the car with strangers, but I'm really tired and don't want to walk the rest of the way. However, I'm afraid that if I make a run for it again, he might chase me down the street or do something worse. Out of fear and panic, I get into the man's car.

"See, I'm not going to bite you," he says, smiling. "I'm an entrepreneur, and I run my own business. I'm a cool guy.

What's the address?"

"Um, it's on Peacock Street, a few blocks down," I lie.

There's no way I'm gonna give this man my real address, but it will at least be close enough for me to walk the rest of the way home. He begins to drive the car slowly.

"You seem like a nice girl, not like a hoe," he tells me.

I'm still experiencing shock throughout my body. All I can think about is my life ending. He's going to drive off and kidnap me! Why did I get in this car? What was I thinking?

"I guess you're right," I say, steadying my voice as best as I can. I squeeze my legs together as tightly as possible as I stare at him, watching his every move.

"I think you're a pretty girl. I would like to get to know you more. We can hang out, and I can pay you for it," he tells me, looking at the road and then looking over at me.

"What do you mean by pay me to hang out?" I ask, confused.

We are approaching the street I told him to drop me off at.

"You know, we hang out, we'll have sex, and I'll pay you for it," he admits.

"Oh, okay," I say, trying not to show my panic and fright.

He stops the car, gets out a pen and paper, writes his number down, and hands it to me.

"I'll give you a call. Here's my street. Thanks for the ride," I tell him with a fake smile on my face.

"Sure thing. Anytime," he says, staring at my thighs and then at me.

I open the car door and get out slowly, looking at him from my side view. To my surprise, he doesn't reach for me and allows me to leave his car in one piece. I close the door and begin walking straight until he drives off. Once I see he's no longer in the area. I turn around and sprint to the street where my house is.

"Thank God I made it out alive! Don't ever do anything stupid like that again!" I say to myself.

I have three more weeks to endure before I go to college—just three more.

As the days start dwindling, I'm getting nervous about finding a college roommate. I haven't heard anything from the university about setting me up in a dorm. A close friend told me that if the school runs out of dorm space, I may be left to find a college apartment with a roommate. This was taking a toll on my mental health. With working crazy shifts at the restaurant with no help from managers, dealing with parent issues at home, and catching the lusting eyes of men, I'm starting to feel like I might be stuck in this place forever.

Everything changed the last week of summer, just before the school year started. I was working the front counter at the restaurant when a girl wearing a shirt with my college name on it came in to order food. Her hair was long, sandy brown, and complimented her yellow skin that seemed to glisten without sunlight. She was a natural beauty, with big brown eyes that caught the eye of the male employees watching. She was petite but shapely, with a soft and gentle voice. I gazed at her the entire time while she told me her order, staring as if I was mesmerized.

"That will be it," she tells me.

"Cool, that will be $10.48," I inform her.

She begins reaching into her purse, and I sense the need to know more about her attending the same college as me a week from now.

"Excuse me!" I interrupt. "You're wearing a University shirt. Are you going to be a freshman there because I'm incoming and looking for a roommate?"

She hands me the money, then glares at me, smiling. She's staring at me as if she likes what she sees.

"Yeah! I'm a sophomore looking for a roommate to live with me in a new college apartment, " she says excitedly.

"Okay! That sounds great! Have you found a roommate yet?" I ask her.

I'm praying that she hasn't so I can be her roommate. I'm just going to come out and say she's a baddie indeed, but most importantly, she seems friendly and could possibly be a good person to room with.

She glares down at her phone for a quick minute, then stares back at me.

"No, I haven't! If you want to stay with me, I can give you my number and more information. My name is Myesha," she says, smiling.

"Myesha, it's nice to meet you! I'm DJ! I will text you about rooming. Thank you so much!" I say excitedly.

A male worker calls her order and hands her the food, squinting at her greedily. She grabs the bag from him without paying his eyes any mind and directs her eyes back at me.

"Well, I'll see you soon, DJ! Just remember to text me," she tells me firmly.

"I will! Thank you again!" I say happily.

I can't believe I just found a roommate out of the blue like this, especially a baddie roommate. I feel like this college thing will work out for me. It's exciting! I'm excited now more than ever!

"She was bad as hell! You know that girl?" a male employee asks me.

"No, but I do now. She gave me her number," I say, boasting to him as I wave the paper she wrote her number on in his face. He looks at me and starts laughing as he returns to his station.

"You guys think y'all the only one who can get girls' numbers, huh!" I say in response to his laughing.

The end of the week has come, and my mom and sister are carrying my boxes to the back of the SUV. I spent the last two nights reflecting on my high school years and the friendships I will soon leave behind.

Just two days ago, my boyfriend from sophomore year reached out to me and wanted to meet, and like an idiot, I did. We went to the park just to chill and talk about moving on to better things. When he dropped me back off at home, he leaned in to get a kiss, but I pulled back quickly and told him that our relationship had been over since the month he wanted to take a break. He cheated on me with one of his homegirls.

His face fell flat as I jumped out of the car, and he drove off without looking back. I knew that would be the last time I would see him again. I could feel my heart dropping from a skyscraper, but I'm relieved to be finally moving on.

"Can you grab your mirror and put it in the car carefully?" my mom demands.

"Yes, I will right now!" I respond.

I grab a bag full of my high school sports trophies in track and volleyball and grab my mirror as directed. The day is sad for some reason, with gray clouds beginning to form in the sky. The wind is powerful, blowing the unwilling leaves right and left.

"Let's hurry up and beat this weather before it beats us," my mom commands both my sister and me.

We get everything I need in the car and take off into the streets. I look out the window and see a typical day in this place: men on the corner, liquor stores, gang members, and drug dealers in disguise. I won't miss this place at all. I won't miss the constant fighting to protect myself, the lusty eyes from neighborhood men, the long walks from work, and the harassment by the police. I don't know what college will be, but I assume it has to be better than this. Anything is better than this.

We get on the highway, and the GPS says it will take us two hours to get to the college apartment where I will live with my new roommate, Myesha, and two other girls.

Myesha and I have talked more since I took her order that day. I feel comfortable moving in with her, but it made me nervous when she said the place was a 4-bedroom. I'm nervous about these two other girls. Are they going to be like the girls back home? The ones who always have an attitude and make something out of nothing? Will they not like me for stupid reasons like how I dress or how my body is shaped?

We begin to pass a lot of farmland and trees, and I realize this may be the opposite of what I'm used to. What if the other roommates are white? I have never lived with white people before. I've had white friends who were cool, but I also felt ostracized by white people in public. I don't want to make them feel uncomfortable, or worse—they make me feel uncomfortable. What will this college experience be? Forget the roommates. What about friends? I'm not living on campus like most freshmen this school year. Myesha said she is a sophomore; will everybody else be upperclassmen? How will I meet people like me if I'm not in a dorm?

A sick feeling starts to hit my stomach. I won't be able to make friends because I live off campus and will be alone every day. I should have never accepted Myesha's offer to be her roommate. I could hang out with her, but what if she already has friends she talks to? All of these thoughts start pouring into my brain. The closer we get to the school, the more my insecurities grow.

My mind is still racing as we make it into town and to the college apartment I will be living in. There are other students and their parents everywhere, unloading boxes and moving furniture up staircases and into rooms. I get out of the car and head up to the third floor of my building, where my apartment and potentially three other girls await. I open the door, and there is no one else there yet. I examine the area. The kitchen is pretty nice, with bar lights and dark brown cabinets. The living room has a long, sandy brown couch with a 32-inch TV meant for sharing. I go to my assigned room, and it's bigger than my entire room back home.

There is a queen-size bed with black dressers on each side of the room. I open the door to the right of me, and it's my bathroom! I have never had my own bathroom! I start to smile uncontrollably at the sight of this. There's a huge mirror and a decent-size tub just for me. This is unbelievable! I'm feeling super pumped off the bathroom alone. My mom and sister make it up the steps with a few boxes.

"Okay! This is nice! Is anybody home?" my mom yells, releasing the box from her arm.

"No, I don't think anyone is home yet, but I hope soon," I say as I run out of the place and down the stairs to help collect my things.

It took a good 30 minutes to unpack everything from the car and an extra 20 minutes to take a break from the stairs, which caused us all to breathe extremely heavily. Once every box is in the apartment, I am responsible for unloading and decorating because my mom and sister have to return to town for work in the morning.

"You're all grown up now," my mom says as she drops the last box off. She shifts her eyes around the apartment and then stares at me.

My eyes begin to water as I see her sadness. I feel all my insecurities hit me at once.

"Come here, give me a hug," she says with a soft voice.

I don't speak. I just go over and hug her tightly. Tears begin to roll down my eyes and spill on my cheeks.

"What am I doing here?" I ask myself in my head.

I'm leaving my family—the life I know for a life I have no clue how to live. Yes, my life is hard, but I'm a hard worker, and maybe I'm stepping out of line by coming to a place like this.

I wipe the tears from my eyes before letting my mother go, and my sister comes right after her.

"Be safe and call us if anything goes wrong," my sister tells me.

"Okay, I will. Make sure y'all drive safely," I say, escorting them out the door and to the car.

Before my mom gets in the car, she comes to me for another hug and tells me I will do fine on my own because I have already been on my own. I agree and tell her not to worry about me. She gets in the car, honks the horn, and drives off.

Once I no longer see her car, I cry out loud. I wipe the tears and head back up the stairs into my apartment. I look at all the boxes I have to unpack, but I can only see my mom. I look around the empty apartment and realize I'm alone. I cry softly, this time as I sit on the floor and begin unpacking each box.

Chapter Two:
BUS STOP

The first week of school has started, and just like I predicted, I'm alone 24/7. My other roommates are friendly, so that's a plus, but they're party girls. They're never at home. Myesha has spent her whole life at this school, so she's out and about reconnecting with friends from last year and partying like the rest of them. I've never been a party person, not even in high school, because I always had to work. Besides school dances, I was never invited to parties. I spent most of my time at home listening to music in the dark and writing poems about my bottled-up feelings.

I have an 8 a.m. class today, so I wake up early to fix my hair and choose my outfit carefully. Everyone on campus is so stylish, and I can't keep up with the hype. The girls are beautiful, and each of their hair follicles is perfect. The guys are popular and out of my league.

I straighten my hair and put on light sweatpants with a basic T-shirt. No matter how hard I try, I look like a tomboy—feminine but rough around the edges. I've always dressed this way because I lived the same life as my older brother. I look at the clock, and it's time for me to get on the apartment shuttle bus to campus. I grab my backpack and a quick snack out of the refrigerator before I head down to get the 7:45 a.m. bus, hoping to make it to class on time.

There aren't many kids who take this bus, and I like it because I get to be myself without feeling like someone's watching or my hair is being stared at by onlookers who constantly compare themselves to others. I have my headphones in, listening to the same music I listened to back home.

As the bus pulls up on the main road, I examine the beauty of the campus. The "Greek Town" area is a neighborhood with tall plantation-like houses with different decorations and letters hanging from the roof. There are many girls and guys from afar who all look identical with the same hair, clothes, and voice. The campus has several brick buildings with students everywhere, going in each direction. There are all types of people here: athletes, cool kids, geeks, music kids, freshmen, and then there's me.

The student center is a colossal tan building with many different places for students. There are places to eat, a huge bookstore that sells everything, including your soul, and many places to sit. I notice that most black students sit in a specific area in the student center, like the cool kids in high school who sit in the lunch cafeteria.

I finally make it to my class, and there is a line out the door. Assuming it's for attendance, I get in line and wait to sign my name on the login sheet. A girl is standing in front of me with long black hair and hoop earrings that match the color of her shirt. Her outfit looks like she is going to an outing at 8 a.m.

She turns to glance at me, and I hurry and look away to avoid awkward eye contact.

"Oh shit! Dj?" the girl questions me excitedly. I look at her face to figure out how she knew my name, a nickname at that.

"Tasha? From middle school?" I say back at her in disbelief.

Tasha and I were good friends in middle school before she transferred to a different high school at the end of the year. She looks fully grown and has lost a little weight since then.

"Yes! Girl, I ain't seen you in hellas! We have the same class!" she says in relief as if she was looking for a person to call a friend.

I can sense my body lighting up inside because I finally met someone I know! I won't have to be so lonely anymore!

"Yeah! This is crazy!" I say with excitement.

We sign our names on the sheet and sit next to each other in class. We discuss what happened after middle school and if there are any special guys in our lives. I tell her I don't have a special person in my life right now, and she laughs aloud.

"You've always been funny! I swear, boy," she replies as the professor begins to look our way.

After class, she tells me about her meal plan with the school, and says that I can eat with her anytime. We go to one of the dining halls to eat and catch up, and I feel like a freshman on campus. In the course of our conversation, I gather that Tasha lives in the dorm; she is also alone.

"There's this freshman event happening tonight on campus. You should come and hang out with me," she tells me with a serious face.

"Yeah, okay. I'll try to make it," I reply, walking away to catch my apartment shuttle home.

I get on the shuttle bus and smile at the thought of hanging with Tasha while staring out the window. For once, I have something to look forward to. This freshman party is exactly what I need to meet more people like me and hang out with Tasha. I get off the bus and run up the steps to my apartment. Myesha is there, getting ready for what looks like her first class.

"Hey! Got any plans tonight?" Myesha says to me as I open the door.

She must have recognized that I have no friends and have spent most of my time alone in the apartment.

"Um, I just met with my friend, and there's a freshman event tonight. She wants me to go with her," I reply.

She looks at me with a big smile.

"That's great! I was just going to invite you to come with me and my friends to a kickback tonight, but you should go with your friend," she nicely tells me, relieved that I finally have one friend on campus.

"Thanks! Maybe another time. I would love to hang out!" I say, hoping to keep receiving future invites.

"No problem. Have fun tonight!" she responds while walking out the door.

I go to my room and into my bathroom, where I look at myself in the mirror. I begin jumping up and down and singing lyrics to an unknown song. I'm happy about tonight!

"What is a kickback?" I say to myself. I am out of the know about this college party stuff.

I begin prancing around and touching my hips, thinking about how I can flaunt my natural curves. My phone buzzes, and I receive a text from Tasha telling me to meet her on campus at 8 p.m. It finally dawns on me that I don't have a car to get to campus now.

Feeling disappointed at this realization, I hurry down to the leasing office to ask if the shuttle bus runs after hours. However, the office is closed. A flyer on the door reads, "Trying to get to campus? The bus will arrive in front of the office!"

"Yes!" I say to myself in relief. I may be able to go after all.

I rush back to the apartment and dig through my closet to find something pretty to wear. I'm going to try to look like the other girls on campus. I take my speaker and blast some popular rap music to get me going. I am smiling and feeling energetic about how the night will go.

I should wear a tight dress or leggings with a crop-top shirt. My hips are round, and all the guys back home always call me thick. I want to look thick tonight.

The night finally comes. I am dressed in a cute crop top and black leggings that have a white stripe down the leg. I decided that cute and casual would be the best outfit since it was going to be my first night on campus.

I message Tasha to let her know I am waiting for the bus and will let her know when I arrive. I grab my bag, check my hair in the mirror for the 80th time, and head for the bus. The night is warm, which is a good sign because I won't need a jacket, so my outfit won't get messed up.

I'm waiting on the bus the flyer claims will show up for me. The time hits 8:10 p.m., and the bus hasn't arrived yet. I begin to worry inside. All this dress-up will be for nothing if I can't attend the party. I can't spend another night alone like I have for the past week. I look down at my phone, and Tasha texts me, asking if I have got on the bus already. Ignoring her text, I scroll through my contacts and stop at Myesha's number. The invite to the kickback may still be on the table. I look at her name but don't press any buttons.

I hear footsteps coming toward me, and I immediately shape up and peek out into the distance. A guy is coming out of the darkness and into the light of the leasing office. As he comes closer, I see his face. He has these huge brown eyes, a big nose, and big full lips. He is light-skinned and over 6 ft. I look away from him to avoid awkwardness, but I can sense his big brown eyes staring at me willingly.

I look over at him to see that he is still staring, and we catch eyes. I immediately feel weird and glance at my phone for anything to save me. He wears a light gray jacket, sweatpants, and a nice top. I look again, and he looks down for a moment. I stare at his side profile. His dark brown facial hair hangs a little over his chin. His hands are in his pockets, and his eyes are focused and still. He must be waiting on this imaginary bus, just like me. He moves his head up and begins staring at me again.

"Hey! Do you know when this bus is supposed to come?" I say, breaking the silence.

"Uh, nah, I don't know. I'm waiting for some friends to pick me up. You trying to get to campus?" he asks me, moving in closer, happy that I had invited him for a talk. He starts smiling at me now.

"Yes, I am, but this fake-ass flyer said a bus was coming, but I realize it's not," I tell him, trying to lighten the mood.

He laughs as he looks down at my outfit choice.

"What's your name? Where you from?" he asks me in a smooth, baritone voice as if he wants to know who I am.

"My name is DJ, and I'm from St. Louis. Where you from?" I ask.

He's standing in front of me, directly in the light; his eyes are melting into mine, and they match the warmth of his skin.

"I'm from Chicago, the best city in the world. I can tell you from the Lou. You got that accent," he says, looking into me with the cutest smile.

I laugh out loud.

"Accent? What accent? Everyone has been telling me that," I respond, staring at him. He is lean, and that's something I like.

"I can just tell. Do you live in these apartments? You a sophomore?" he asks me.

We are now playing 20 questions.

"Yeah, I live here, but I'm a freshman," I tell him.

"For real! That's cool! I'm a sophomore, but this is my first year at this school," he informs me, still glaring straight in my eyes.

That's cool too!" I say, staring directly into his eyes.

He sees the smile on my face and bites his lips on the side.

"Well, if you ever want to hang out, here's my number," he says.

He reaches for my phone and asks me to unlock it. He makes a funny face; I laugh and unlock it for him. He puts his number in my phone and tells me his name is Tomo. He tells me not to hesitate to hit him up to hang. I tell him I'll take him up on his offer. Suddenly, headlights shine into the darkness, and it's not the bus. It's his friends.

"Hey! Call me, and I'll see you around, okay," he says, looking at me with flirty eyes.

"I got you!" I say as I smile uncontrollably.

He eats my smile, gets into the car with his friends, and they drive off roughly.

Smiling ear to ear, I run back to my apartment building. For some reason, I don't mind spending this night alone anymore. I text Tasha to let her know that I won't make it and that I'll see her tomorrow. The energy I felt with Tomo was weird but familiar. He's cute and tall and kind of a vibe. His eyes are so big. Why did he stare straight into my soul the entire time? Maybe he was feeling me? All of these questions appear in my head.

"Are you going to hang with him?" I ask myself in my head, looking at his phone number.

"I guess," I whisper to myself.

I hear the front door moving and immediately snap back into normal mode. It's Myesha. She is dressed up and looks beautiful as usual.

"Hey, girl! Are you not going to the party anymore?" she asks me with a confused look.

"I forgot the bus isn't running, and I don't have a car to get to campus," I remind her.

She looks at me with a slight frown on her face. "You want to come to this kickback I'm about to go to?" she re-offers.

I know she feels sorry for me and wants to help however she can.

"Yes! I'll go! Thanks!" I respond.

She smiles and tells me to give her one minute before we head out.

This has turned out to be a good night, after all.

Chapter Three:

MY PLACE

I t's two weeks into the school year, and Tasha and I hang out every day after classes. She swipes me in for food at the student dining halls, and we feast and talk about everything. I tell her about the weird but cute guy I met at the bus stop, and she wants to know all the details.

She picks up her fork full of lasagna noodles and stuffs it in her mouth. She wasn't playing when she said she was hungry after her second class.

"It's not weird! Just hit him up like, 'Hey, you wanna hang out this week?'" she instructs me.

"I guess. I just never hit a dude up like, 'Hey, you wanna come over to my place?'" I tell her as I finish my chicken pasta.

"You're bound to see him again anyway," she says.

"True. I'll just text right now and ask," I say, scrolling through my contact list to Tomo.

I am so nervous doing this. What if he doesn't respond? I would look so stupid. What if he has a girlfriend or something? What if Homeboy is a player looking for his next idiot to play? I stopped assuming and just texted his number.

I put my phone down and look at Tasha, who loves this drama.

"I'm gonna go get some more pasta," I tell her.

There's no way I can sit here in anticipation, staring at my phone, waiting for him to text me back. I walk to the pasta station, wondering if I'm moving too fast. I officially cut off my ex from high school a month ago, and I'm already sweating over some guy I just met at a bus stop. Lost in thought, I fill my plate with more than I can eat and return to the table.

"Your phone lit up!" proclaimed Tasha with a big smile.

"Girl, you are more excited than I am!" I tell her, putting my plate down and reaching for my phone.

I look down at the message, which reads, 'Hey, wassup! We can hang out. What are you doing tonight?'

I start smiling like crazy on the inside, but on the outside, Tasha only sees a little smirk on my face.

"What did he say?" she asked impatiently.

"He asked me what I'm doing tonight," I tell her.

Her face lights up as she looks over at me.

"See, he wants to hang with you! Now reply, you ain't doing nothing," she tells me.

Why is she treating me like I ain't never dealt with a dude before? This ain't my first rodeo, and I'm not even a virgin.

"Okay, I will. Let's hurry and get out of here."

When I get home, my room is messy, so I need to tidy things up before Tomo comes over. This will be the first time I invite a guy to my place. In high school, I would sneak out to my boyfriend's house. I never invited boys to my place because I couldn't. Now, here I am, inviting boys over. I can hear my mom saying I'm too grown up in my head. Where is my life going?

I feel so anxious and nervous. I hope my roommates won't be home. What are we even going to do? Will he just want to go straight to my room? I emptily stare at the hangers in my closet and try to answer these questions. I'm not about to have sex without at least knowing him for a few months. I've never had a one-night stand, and I'm not about to start now.

I hear my phone buzz, and Tomo tells me he's about one minute away. My throat begins to swell up. This is literally about to happen—he's about to be here. I start thinking of the first things I'm going to say. I run to the mirror and make sure I look good.

There's a knock, knock, knock at the front door. I smile, take a deep breath, and go for the doorknob. I open it, and there he is, tall and staring at me with those big brown eyes.

"Hey!" I say. "Come in. I can show you around a little bit."

He follows me on my little tour as I tell him about my roommates. I glance back and see his eyes following my hips.

"Your roommate is Myesha? Cool! I think I know her," he tells me, looking at her door.

We return to the living room, and he sits by me on the couch. He tells me his family is Nigerian and what it was like growing up in Chicago. I tell him I wouldn't have guessed he was African because he looks like a regular light-skinned guy from my neighborhood.

He stared at me, this time with blank eyes. For a moment, it was quiet between us. I apologized to him, and we began talking again. He slid his arm around my shoulder, staring into my soul with a warm smile.

"You really don't live on campus," he says.

"Yeah, I don't. The school didn't have enough space for me, so here I am."

"Can I hide my drugs here?" he asks.

"What!" I ask, so confused.

"Like, if I ever get caught up, I can hide my drugs here, right?" he tells me with a stupid look on his face. I can tell he's joking.

I smile but give him a weird stare.

"No, I won't be hiding anything for anybody," I assured him.

He laughs and starts asking me about my interests. Then he pulls out his phone and starts smiling at the screen.

"What are you looking at?" I ask him, wanting to know.

"Are you flexible?" he asks.

"What?" I say, confused again.

"Like, can you do a split?" he elaborates.

"What are you talking about?" I say, alarmed.

This dude can't be serious with these questions.

He comes in closer and shows me his phone with a picture of a girl with a big butt and a hand gripping her butt underneath.

"Is this you? You look like you got that grip," he tells me, looking at the phone and then at my thighs.

"Wow!" I say.

"Are you serious right now?" I scream, looking directly into his eyes."

He takes on the challenge, laughing and smiling while staring back into mine.

"I'm just playing with you, girl," he warns me, then says smoothly, "But you are cute and thick." He stares at me and slides his right hand on my upper leg.

I peep his hand placement and instantly get up, making an excuse to go to my room. When I move, he follows me.

"Look, I'm sorry. I don't mean any harm. I'm a virgin, so there's nothing to worry about," he tells me.

I look back and stare at him with a straight face.

"So, you're a virgin, but you're asking me all these questions related to sex? That doesn't make any sense!" I yell at him, looking for an honest answer to my question.

He looks at me with shifting eyes and walks close behind me.

"Yes. I never had sex with a girl. I'm a virgin. You seem cool. I'm just playing with you with the questions," he assures me.

He grabs my hips from the back and presses his body into mine. I remain still as he touches my shoulder with his chin and breathes into my neck. He smells so good, and his breath is warm on my skin. I feel his hands gripping my hips.

"Let's go into your room and chill real quick," he says, using the softest voice in my ear.

Things have just turned real. It went from joking to him touching my body and breathing on my neck. I begin to think about the last time I had sex, and it's been a long time since I felt like this. I don't like how he came on to me, but I like this feeling. His hands are soft and firm; his smell is pleasant; his voice is deep and soothing.

I let him guide me into my room with our bodies still attached as he closes the door behind us. He puts his weight onto my body, and we fall onto the bed. He releases me and stands up, staring at me. I glance at him up and down as I move the pillow on my bed. I feel weird about what's happening, but I like the energy I'm getting.

"There are so many funny videos I find online. This one is so funny I want to show you," I say, trying to slow down the momentum between us.

"Cool!" he says as he takes off his jacket.

I turn to lie on my stomach with my phone in my face, trying to find the video I want to show him. This position was probably not the best to show that I don't want to have sex, but I don't know what I want to do right now. He begins talking as I feel him lay on top of me and put his hands around my waist. He nudges his head onto my shoulder again and looks at me, his lips just inches away from mine.

Though he is on top of me, he is talking to me as if we were having a normal conversation. This makes me feel comfortable, and I like his body. I begin showing him the videos and telling him why I think it's funny. He laughs, moving his head off my shoulder. The room gets quiet now. All I can hear is the sound of my voice. He begins to press his lower body down on my hips, and I feel his print rubbing down my back.

I stop talking as he softly strokes me from the back, fully clothed. I position myself better as he pulls my hips towards him. First, he starts slow, then he begins to stroke me hard and strong. I begin to moan and make noise. This gets him excited. He starts to go faster and harder, squeezing tighter on my waist.

We are in full clothes-burn mode. The firm grip of his hands on my hips excites me, and it feels as if we are having sex. He stops suddenly, lays flat on top of me, and brings his face onto my shoulder again.

This time, he is breathing heavily, directly into the bend of my neck. This excites me. I start caressing the side of his head.

"You okay?" I ask him.

Tomo smiles, his eyes closed, and continues breathing into my neck. A few seconds pass, and then silence.

"Yeah, I'm good," he says to me in a firm but tired tone.

We lay in silence for a few moments. I can't believe we just had sex with all of our clothes on. Why didn't we just slip them off? Why did this just feel like the real thing? I felt him as if he was inside my body, but he wasn't. Why does he turn me on?

He eventually lifts off me, and I flip myself over. He is standing there fixing his pants as if he took them off in the first place.

I get up, and he stares at me with a satisfied look.

"Um, it's getting late, and I have an early class tomorrow," I tell him, walking out of my room.

He follows me and puts a hand on my hip.

"Yeah. I guess I should go," he says as he pulls me into him.

I stare into his eyes, confused about what happened between us. He looks at me as if he knows what it is.

"I'll see you later," he tells me in a firm, deep voice.

"Okay," I say softly, glancing up at his face. I'm getting lost in his big, smiling eyes.

He lets me go and walks out the front door without looking back at me. I let the door slam behind him as I stood there, lost.

I feel good, but weird. Horny but confused. I don't know what just happened.

Chapter Four:
THE HAPPENSTANCE

The next day, I wake up jaded. All I can think of is last night with Tomo and what we did in this room. I hear my other roommates talking amongst themselves and preparing to go to their classes. Their voices are high-pitched and annoying, interrupting my thoughts. I lean over my dresser and grab my phone to see if he texted me. I look, and there's no text from anyone.

I throw my cover off and amble into the bathroom. I look at myself in the mirror, and my hair is a complete mess. I immediately unwind my flat iron and get to straightening my hair. It must have been messed up from last night's fiasco. I know we didn't have sex, but why is my brain responding as if we did?

I squint my eyes as I search the countertop for my glasses, which is hard because I need my glasses to find my glasses. I finally find them and put them on my face. The lenses are smudged, and I can see the smoke coming from my hair. It's my fourth time straightening my hair this week, so I know I'm bound to get heat damage. Ignoring this fact, I continue to straighten. As I finish, my phone buzzes, and I run to see who it is.

It's Tasha. She's asking if I'm coming to class today.

"Duh! Of course, I'm coming to class!" I say out loud to the message.

I responded with a yes, feeling slightly disappointed that it wasn't Tomo. I don't know if I want to see him again after last night, but he should say something to me, right?

Ignoring my question, I scatter through my closet and choose the easiest outfit to be on time for class.

I go into the kitchen to quickly eat a bowl of cereal before I head out. Myesha comes out of her room with messy hair and dressed in her pajamas.

"Hey girl, you going to class?" she asks me, walking to the refrigerator.

"Yeah, I got an early one today, but I'm just so tired," I say while sloppily eating my cereal.

"That sucks! What did you do last night?" she asks as a conversation starter.

I stop myself from telling her the weird experience I had with Tomo last night.

"Um, I met this guy named Tomo. He says he knows you. Do you know him?" I ask her.

"Maybe. How does he look?" she asks me.

At this point, I know his look all too well.

"Tall, light skin, Nigerian from Chicago. He lives here; he's a sophomore."

She looks up at the ceiling and thinks of who he could be.

"I'm not sure if I know who he is. Maybe you could invite him over one day," she tells me.

I shoot her with a crazy look. If only she knew he was already here, looking at her door and pounding against my hips.

"Yeah. Maybe," I reply as I finish my bowl and put it in the sink.

"Well, let me know. Have a good day on campus!" she tells me, waving as I storm out the door.

I get on the shuttle bus and put my headphones in automatically. I search the seats to see if Tomo is on the bus. He is not here, and a part of me is relieved. I begin thinking of what I will say to him the next time I see him. What would you say to a person you clothes-burned with for the first time if they were not your boyfriend? I don't even know if I would consider it a one-night stand. He said he was a virgin. Maybe he was afraid to have sex. But his strokes and movements were on point as if he were a dude with experience. What if the virgin thing is just a lie?

I get off the shuttle and tell Tasha to save me a seat while I jog across campus and into the right building. Tasha has saved my seat, and I'm breathing hard as my forehead begins to sweat.

"Dang girl, you okay?" Tasha asks with a concerned voice.

"Yeah, I'm cool," I reply, slamming my backpack on the ground while sliding into the mini seat they call a desk.

The row of students behind us gives me an annoyed look as Tasha continues to talk to me.

"Is the reason you were late something to do with you and that guy last night?" she beams excitedly.

She now looks directly at me, smirking, patiently waiting for my answer. I take out my notebook and begin jotting down the notes I missed from the starting minutes of class.

"Well?" Tasha asks, her face is now straight and impatient.

As I'm writing, I'm thinking of telling a lie. There's no way I will tell her I clothes-burned with this random guy I met a week ago. That's so embarrassing!

"We just hung out. He asked me some crazy questions, which caught me off guard," I finally respond.

"So y'all didn't do anything?" she firmly asks, leaving me no room to tell more lies.

"No, girl. Let's talk later."

It was difficult for me to focus throughout the remainder of my classes. I have a Spanish class and a lot of homework to finish by tonight. It's going to be a long day.

Tasha and I follow our routine, heading to the campus dining hall for lunch. This time, we walk the extra mile to the dining hall, known for having the best food on campus. We fill our plates with more than enough food and find a booth with some sunlight to talk about boy drama one-on-one. She has a boyfriend she's been dating since high school, and he's been up to no good.

"You know you're gonna have to give me all the details," Tasha reminds me as we begin digging into our plates.

My head begins to narrow down the details of last night, only preparing the details that would not make me look like a total idiot.

"When he got to my place, he kept staring at me all crazy. Tomo started asking me questions like am I flexible? Can he hide his drugs at my place? He was touching my thighs, too!" I tell her.

Tasha's face turns bright red. She's so thrilled about this drama she looks as if she is about to explode.

"Bitch! What did he ask you!? I can't believe he would do that!" she says with her eyes wide open.

"Yeah, it was crazy, but he said he was just playing, and supposedly, he's a virgin," I tell her, putting air quotes around the virgin part.

"These dudes are crazy!" she says, squeezing ketchup over her fries. "What's the point of him telling you he's a virgin? You weren't trying to have sex with him anyway." She looks up to my eyes to confirm if what she said was true.

"Hell, nawl!" I respond. "I barely know the dude; he could have a whole girlfriend or something."

I begin to question this thought more now than ever. What if he does have a girlfriend, and instead of having sex with other girls, he clothes-burns with them?! That way, he can technically say he's not cheating on her.

I begin eating my food while Tasha explains why she suspects her boyfriend might be cheating.

After our talk, we both decide we have too much homework and should get to it. She tells me about a party happening over the weekend. I give her a maybe and say I'd text her later.

Luckily, I catch the last shuttle bus from campus and return to my college apartment. Turning the corner, I see my building and a person standing at the front door.

It's Tomo! He is wearing a crispy white T-shirt and black pants. He looks straight ahead as if someone is about to open the door. I sprint up the staircase, hoping none of my roommates are home. When I reach the top of the stairs, he immediately looks my way. He has a straight face, but his eyes are smiling.

"What in the world are you doing?" I yell at him as I move in front of the door and into his face.

He starts to smile wide, staring into my eyes. I'm beginning to think this is his favorite thing to do.

"I wanted to see you," he says in a deep voice. He extends his arms out, grabs my hips, and pulls me closer to him.

"No, no, no! If you wanted to see me, you would text and let me know you were coming, not just show up! I wasn't even home!" I berate him.

I pull away from his grip and turn to open the front door.

At this moment, I decided to give Tomo a nickname: Stalker.

"Come in. We need to talk real quick," I demand.

He shakes his head and mimics my words as he strides through the door, feeling comfortable.

I take his hand like a child, guiding him directly to my room, and shut the door. He senses that I'm upset, yet he pushes me on the wall and slams his body up on mine. His face is only an inch away as he takes his hands and places them right on my hips. His eyes are large, and they begin searching my face.

I'm so frustrated right now! Who does he think he is? Stalker pinning me to this wall is taking me back to my high school when the guys would pin girls to their lockers, and the only way to get the guys off is to play fight.

This is what we begin to do.

I grab his arms and throw them off of me. He stumbles back, and I push him toward the opposite wall.

"Get off of me," I demand. "I'm not in a good mood right now."

He looks at me, startled, then with feisty eyes as he realizes what's happening.

"Make me," he says in his deep voice as he walks back over to me with his arms opened wide.

We begin to play fight all over the room. Pushing, hitting, pulling, grabbing and touching.

A few minutes pass, and we end up back in the same position on the wall. Stalker has me pinned, with my hands in the air while his hands secure mine. We are both breathing heavily and are a little sweaty.

He stares into me as if he wants to eat me alive. I look at him as if I want him to eat me up. At this point, I want him to kiss me, but I'm not sure if he'll get the clue. I begin biting my lips and smiling my eyes at him.

"What do you wanna do now?" he mumbles in a distorted voice. He lets my hands go and slides his hands down to my hips, beginning to caress me.

"You tell me," I say softly to him.

My eyes are smiling so hard at him. My lips tremble as I wait for him to lean in and give them a French kiss.

"Can I ask you something?" he says to me.

The whole time, his eyes never leave mine. My hips begin to feel more relaxed the more his hands massage me.

"Yes!" I say excitedly.

What could he possibly want to ask at this moment? We shouldn't even be talking right now. It should be nothing but action taking place. His body on mine, my body on his, our lips tangled up.

"Can I kiss you?" he says to me in a nervous voice.

"What?" I question. "Of course, you can kiss me! You don't even have to ask me," I affirm to him.

"I didn't know if you would be down for it," he says, moving his hands from my thighs onto my waist.

Why would he ask this question? The play fighting, the clothes burning from the other night, the way I'm looking at him right now, why didn't he pick up on all of these signs that read, "I like you, and I want you to kiss me."

He smiles wide once he hears that I'm okay with it.

"I am," I say in a soft voice.

This is awkward. Now, we're looking at each other, waiting to kiss. I wish he had just kissed me instead of asking because now I know he's about to. He hesitates, so I slide my arms around his neck and press his head into mine. Stalker follows my movement, leaning closer to my face and shifting his eyes to my lips, eyes, and nose until our lips finally lock.

Once his lips meet mine, I begin sticking my tongue in his mouth, pressing on the inside of his lips. I feel like I'm his dentist. He follows my every move as our heads begin twisting and turning into each other, our noses start dancing, and our lips begin making little noises. I can feel his hands rubbing down my chest and to my waist the more we kiss. I can tell he is not a natural good kisser, but he is copying my movements.

I slowly lean out of the kiss, and he follows. His eyes are smaller than usual, and he smiles at me again. I smile back at them.

"That was fire," Stalker says in a satisfied voice.

I tug on his arms so he can let me go. He releases me as I turn from the wall to sit on the bed.

He follows and turns towards me, standing.

"Do you have a girlfriend?" I finally ask.

"Girlfriend?" he questions.

"I wouldn't be here right now if I had a girlfriend," he assures me.

He turns and sits next to me on the bed. He stares at me, but I do not turn to do the same.

"What do you want from me?" I ask him. I turn my body towards him as I look dead into his eyes for the answer.

I don't understand what you mean?" he says, squinting with a confused face.

"I mean, we getting all touchy and whatever, so are you looking for sex, or are you feeling me?" I ask him.

He begins laughing out loud, but I am not laughing.

"I mean, we are just chilling; we're friends," he says.

Last time I checked, the guys I called friends don't make out with me, almost have sex with me, and are completely turned on by me. Not to mention, they don't usually show up at my house uninvited.

He stands up from where he's sitting on my bed and looks at me, waiting for my response.

"I mean, last time I checked, friends didn't do what we just did. I'm all down with being friends and doing friendly things," I say, looking at him to see his reaction.

He begins laughing out loud again. I don't know what's funny with what I said.

"We are friends," he says again.

For some reason, I don't think this is the last time our bodies will touch.

"Cool. Well, I gotta get to the library and finish some Spanish homework, so you gotta go," I say.

"You don't have to tell me twice," he says, smirking.

I direct him out of my room and to the front door. He jokes around with me, and I laugh at his words. I tell him I'll catch up with him some other time, and he laughs and pulls me in to hug him.

"Bye, friend!" he jokes while heading out the door.

I grab my backpack and fix my hair, which is messed up again after dealing with Stalker.

I put on my slides and walk out of my apartment door. I trip down several steps and head toward the back of the leasing office, where residents have access to a 24-hour gym, computer room, and many study rooms.

I go into the computer room and slam my backpack on the ground. There is a guy in here. He watches me as I slam my back into the rolling chair. Once I am comfortable, I look back at the guy to see if I have seen him before. He is skinny with dark brown skin. His eyes are big and hazel, and his arms and legs are slumped over the chair he sits on.

I look away to sign into the computer and log in to the Spanish homework I dread to finish. I can write it okay, but I can't understand and speak it to save my life. I put my headphones in and listen to my first audio assignment. The lady is speaking Spanish as fast as lightning! I just don't want to do this homework right now. I distract myself by looking back at the guy at his computer. His eyes are smiling, and he seems to be looking at me from the corner of his eye.

I feel some energy with this guy—a positive one! I'm not attracted to him physically, but he looks like a cool dude to meet. I'm huge on zodiac signs, and I happen to be a Gemini. This may sound ridiculous, but other Geminis can tell if someone else is a Gemini based on looks and intellectual connection. I can sense that this guy is a Gemini like me.

He is full-on gazing at me with a smile on his face. I turn around and catch his eye.

"Hey! Do you happen to be a Gemini by any chance?" I ask him.

He takes both of his earbuds out and fully faces me from across the room.

"Wow! I am actually! How did you know?" he asked.

He gets up from his chair and walks to the chair beside me. Sitting in the chair, he puts his hands on his chin and looks at me inquisitively.

"It's a Gemini thing, I guess. I can tell when someone else is a Gemini because we're awesome!" I say excitedly.

He gazes at me like a puzzle that needs to be solved.

"It's funny you say that because I saw you when you came in and threw your things down, and I sensed something. I couldn't figure out what it is, but now I know!" he says with a cheery face.

I laugh at the face he makes.

"My name is Marcus; I'm an Engineering senior. What about yourself?" he asks.

His voice sounds clear, like the head announcer for the news. He speaks articulately.

"My name is DJ, and I'm a freshman," I respond.

Marcus' eyes grow big after I speak. His mouth drops wide open as if he had just seen the best magic trick of his life.

"You're a freshman!   How in the world did you end up here in these apartments!?" he asks me in shock.

We both begin smiling and facing each other in amazement. I tell him my long story, and he seems impressed with me. He leans into my space, intrigued by my experience and intellect.

"Wow! So you're navigating living amongst upperclassmen, and you just got here, and you're from St. Louis? I know you've seen a lot. How has growing up there made you who you are today?" he asks with an interested face.

This is a heavy question. I can't believe he wants to know where I'm from. Most guys ask me if I have a boyfriend and when they can chill, but not Marcus. He wants to know the real me and why I am the way I am.

I spend the next three hours talking to Marcus about space, spirituality, church, and the funny videos I find online. The entire conversation feels like I am in a different place than I am. I forget about my Spanish homework and focus more on the wisdom coming out of Marcus' mouth. He has a lot of thoughts about everything and has experienced more than I can imagine. His voice is crisp and kind, and they match his wide and relaxed eyes. It hits 2 a.m., and we decide to head to our apartments.

"I'm sorry for taking all your time. You didn't finish your Spanish homework," Marcus says worriedly.

"It's okay. I'll probably wake up early and finish it. I enjoyed talking to you!" I say, looking at him.

It is dark, and he agrees to walk me to the stairs of my apartment. We exchange numbers. He tells me he is always in the study room and I can join him anytime to work. I tell him I would like to study and talk with him more about life. He smiles as I run up the stairs to my apartment. Once inside, I crash onto my bed.

Chapter Five:
THE DM

The weekend is here, and it's lit! Many fraternities and sororities are throwing club parties and some house parties. Tasha is so excited that she sends me every party flyer she can find about this weekend's events. I start smiling as I rise up from my bed and go into the kitchen to eat breakfast. It's Saturday, and the sun is shining through the blinds. I look at my phone, and there's a text from Marcus.

"Good Morning! Did you ever get your homework done from the other night? If you're not doing anything this afternoon, some friends and I are hanging in the study room if you want to join!" the text reads.

I smile at my phone as Myesha walks into the kitchen, looking at me from across the counter.

"What are we smiling at today?" she says, looking at me up and down. I laugh as I put down my phone.

"It's just a friend wanting to hang out," I tell her, grabbing a bowl from the cabinet.

She smirks as she opens the fridge and grabs a carton of orange juice.

"It wouldn't happen to be that guy you were talking to me about that night, is it?" she asks with curious eyes. She sips the juice and makes a funny face.

"No, not him, it's someone different. He's a cool guy and very smart. More like a study buddy," I assure her as I pour the cereal into my bowl.

She gives me a look and laughs lightly. "A study buddy? If you say so," she says.

For the first time, I ignore her comment.

"So, you going to any parties tonight?" she asks while looking at her phone.

"Yeah, I think I might be going to one of the things happening today. Tasha and I haven't decided which party to go all out for tonight," I tell her.

"Well, I'm about to get ready to go to the mall to see about a cute outfit; if you wanna ride with me?" she offers.

This time, I can't tell if she's trying to include me out of pity or because she needs someone to give a second opinion on her fashion. I agree to go and finish my bowl of cereal.

When we get outside, Myesha opens the door to her shiny silver Dodge Charger. We both get in simultaneously and click our seatbelts like twins. She turns the stereo to the local hip-hop station, and we blast off into the town streets. The town mall is smaller than any mall back home and has only half the stores you would typically see. There aren't many options to find a bomb outfit to wear except at a popular women's clothing store where you can find every college girl.

We walk in, and all the girls and guys turn around to stare at Myesha. I completely understand why. Her hair bounces when she walks, her eyes shine, and her curves dance happily in her jeans. The girls are staring, but their faces are turning upside down. I'm walking beside her, and people see right over me as if I am invisible.

We go to the dress rack, nick-picking until we find the dress colors and fit we want. Myesha picks a mini pink one and holds it up to her shoulders.

"What do you think about this?" she asks me, squinting into my eyes.

"I think it's cute! Maybe add something like a necklace?" I suggest.

"Yeah, I think you're right," she confirms as she walks towards the dressing room.

I continue to search for something in my size. I noticed weeks ago that Myesha's wardrobe has soft colors like pinks, grays, whites, and blues. Why would she ask me about the dress when she knows it looks like everything in her closet? Maybe she wanted my honest opinion, and my insecurities are beginning to show. I flip through the whole rack and find nothing to my liking. I look to the left, and a group of girls are in the jewelry section, discussing which party they will attend tonight.

"I heard all the fraternity brothers will be at the blue party tonight," says a girl with blonde hair and a red shirt.

"Yes! I'm looking for a boo, and he's bound to be there, okay!" her friend responds to her.

"A boo?" I whisper to myself.

This blue party may be the party Tasha and I should go to. Maybe if I dress up and be somebody I'm not, I can find a boo too. I reach for my phone and send Tasha a message confirming the blue party should be our move tonight. I see her text that says she agrees as my eyes beam toward the store's makeup section.

Myesha and I leave the mall and head home to get the rest of our day started. She tells me she has to meet up with some friends for a pre-game that is happening soon. She drops me off at home, and Tasha hits me up about wanting to come to my place to kick it. She is tired of being on campus, and I'm the only one she knows who lives off campus, or what freshmen call a getaway. She takes the city bus to my place, which is about 15 minutes away from her dorm. I open the door, and she is breathing frantically from the flights of steps I have to deal with daily.

"If you're going to be over here, you betta get used to those steps," I tell her, closing the door.

I grab a water bottle from the fridge and hold it up in her face. She looks up with squinted eyes and quickly takes the water bottle.

"Girl! I don't think I can get used to those. It's hella stairs!" she cries to me as she walks over to the couch.

"How do you think I felt when I moved all my stuff here?" I smirk, then change the topic, "What do you wanna do until the party?"

I didn't plan anything for her arrival, and I'm starting to feel bad the more I look at her breathing heavily.

"I don't know. Is anything going on at the apartment complex?" she asks, looking at me with a straight face.

Just then, my phone buzzed. It is Marcus. He informs me that he and his friends are headed to the big study room behind the leasing office.

"Yes! I know what we can do right now," I tell Tasha in excitement.

I remember that I hadn't told her anything about the night I met Marcus, and now would be a good time to fill her in before I threw her into a situation where random people would be around.

Her face lights up as expected when I tell her about that night. She gets up from the couch, her breath returning to normal, and begins shouting in a high-pitched voice.

"Girl! You met another dude already! You got all the juice, huh!?" she asks me sarcastically.

"It's not even like that, and he is like a friend to me," I assure her.

She looks at me up and down with a smirk on her face. I stare back at her with a straight face to let her know nothing is happening between Marcus and me.

"We should go now; they're probably already there," I say.

I grab my jacket and lead us out the door, down the steps, and to the study room.

For some reason, I feel nervous the closer we get to the study room. Marcus mentioned that his other friends would be there, and I can't help but wonder who his other friends are. Are they guys, girls, or maybe his girlfriend, if he has one? What would she think about us if he introduced me to her? Would she assume what everyone else thinks about us even though I've known him for a few days?

We approach the study room and hear multiple voices talking, with music in the background.

"Okay! It sounds like Marcus knows how to throw a party!" Tasha says behind me. She begins snapping her fingers to the base of the music.

I reach for the door, and we walk into the study room. About six guys are standing, conversing with each other. They appear smart and dressed as if they work at an office. Marcus sees me and begins walking up to me, with one of his friends walking beside him. He has a red cup in his hand, and his smile touches each side of the room. I look at his friend, whose face is straight, but his green eyes are smiling at Tasha and me.

"What's going on, DJ!" Marcus shouts as he leans in to hug me.

"Nothing much! This is my friend, Tasha," I tell him and his friend.

Marcus looks at Tasha with big eyes and leans in to hug her.

"Nice to meet you, Ms. Tasha! My name is Marcus, and this is my friend, Alonzo." He points to Alonzo to say something to us.

I'm going to come out and say this. Alonzo is the finest dude I've seen so far at this college! His dreamy green eyes compliment his structured face and golden skin. Not to mention, he is over 6ft.

Tasha looks up into his eyes as he approaches her. She stares at him as if she is meeting a god. He reaches out his hand for a handshake. For a minute, Tasha is completely lost in what's going on.

Alonzo begins to laugh as he reaches for her hand. She finally catches his drift and shakes his hand.

He then averts his eyes to me to do the same. Now it's my time to admire his beauty. I beam into his eyes as he leans in to shake my hand. He is too fine to be keeping things professional with us.

"Nice to meet you ladies! Y'all want something to drink? I can make it," Alonzo asks us. We nod, and he gets up to bartend us something good.

I look around the room and then look up at Marcus.

"You weren't playing when you told me you and your friends kick it often in these study rooms!" I say in shock.

"We are all engineers, and we take most of the same classes, so we are always kicking it with each other," he explains.

We are sitting directly across from each other. Marcus is smiling at me, and I am smiling at him. Alonzo returns with a red cup for Tasha and me, and I look at him to see if he will tell us what it is. He tells us it's a basic Hennessy and soda mix. We laugh and begin drinking even though we're underage. This will be considered the pre-game for tonight's party.

Marcus and I begin talking as if it's just us in the room. We speak of the parties happening tonight, his engineering classes, the places we've visited, and the things we like to do as hobbies. Periodically, I look over at Tasha, who is chatting with Alonzo with a smile. She is rambling, which is something she typically does when she likes someone. I laugh and look back at Marcus, who hasn't taken his eyes off me.

It's 8:30 p.m., and Tasha and I must return to my place to prepare for tonight's blue party.

"Hey guys, this was fun, but we gotta go turn up!" I tell Marcus and Alonzo.

They look at each other, laughing and making funny faces at us. The alcohol is starting to kick in. Tasha and I begin laughing, and everyone in the room starts laughing. We've all become close friends in a matter of 4 hours. Marcus gets up to hug us both, and Alonzo follows, this time with a hug instead of a handshake. They tell us not to turn up too much, and Marcus invites me to study with Alonzo and him tomorrow.

"I'll be there," I say in a slightly tipsy voice.

He laughs and holds the door to the study room open for us. We look back and say goodbye one last time before heading out the door and up the steps to my apartment building.

"Girl, Alonzo was fine as hell!" Tasha tells me as I open the door.

I glance back at her and see her face—it's red, and her eyes are glossy.

"Yeah, he was, I'm not even going to lie," I confirm, and we giggle like little girls.

We walk into my apartment, and it's a full-on girl function! All of my roommates and some of their friends are getting dressed up, drinking, smoking weed, and blasting rap music. Everyone greets us, and Myesha waves at us to come her way. She is wearing the mini pink dress she bought at the mall, and it looks better on her than I could imagine with the dress just held to her shoulders.

"Hey! Y'all want a drink!?" she asks us.

This night is going to be unlike any other. We take the drink, and all the girls come in to toast a good night. Tasha and I take a sip of our drinks and then go to my room to put on our clothes.

"Living off campus is so fun! We wouldn't be able to do none of what we just did in a dorm," Tasha reminds me.

I go into the closet and grab a tight black dress.

"Yeah, you're right! It is fun." I say back to her.

I go into the bathroom to put on my dress to make sure it fits. I keep thinking about what Tasha said. Living off campus may be the best option. I've already met some incredible people, and I'm bound to meet more. We scored free alcohol twice already before going to the party, and I could find a boo tonight.

Once I finish putting on my dress, I take out my makeup bag and begin trying to work magic. I'm not a makeup girl by any means. I take some foundation, cover my face, fill my eyebrows, and apply red lipstick onto my lips. I add a little mascara, and my look is complete. I push up my boobs and touch my hips as I stare at my body in the mirror.

When I open the bathroom door, Tasha is already dressed and is looking into the mirror, fixing her face. At this point, we are both tipsy. She looks at me and gives me a big smile.

"Girl! You look good. Real thick!" she tells me.

We laugh as I begin twerking to music still playing in one of my roommates' rooms. After we finish our drinks, we call an Uber to take us to the party.

Once our Uber arrives on the party street, it reminds me of a big music festival. There are groups of girls and guys everywhere, and people dress up as if there is going to be a contest for the best dress. Even though there's no physical award, the contest is going on in everyone's heads. Tasha and I get into the party line, which is already 30 people deep. The security is checking everyone's ID and making sure any weapons get confiscated. I look behind me, and about 40 more people have joined the line. I awkwardly make eye contact with a girl behind me with a full face of makeup. She mugs me, and I immediately turn around and stumble upon Tasha, who looks back at me and starts laughing.

When we get to security, they make us put our hands in the air and do a 360-degree turn. I can feel the guards checking our bodies as we turn for them.

"Okay. You're good to go," the guard says to me with a smirk on his face.

Tasha and I walk into the party, and without a second passing, our ears boom with blasting music. The air is very dense, and my glasses start to fog up. There are bodies in every direction, and there is barely space to walk through without getting hit by someone dancing. The club is dark, with neon lights flashing at many random angles. Girls checking their makeup and hair through their phones crowd the bar area, snap-chatting videos of their beauty.

Tasha leads us to a good space in the middle of the dance floor, close to the deejay booth, and we start reciting the lyrics of the song that just came on. I feel the base in my chest as I begin throwing my hands up in the air and screaming. I might just lose my voice tonight. Tasha turns to me and begins twerking on my hips, and I grab her by her waist. This catches the attention of a group of guys in the corner.

Enjoying the music, I bend down and start twerking to the beat in a circular motion. Suddenly, I feel a force push up against me. I feel hands grip my waist and begin pounding me from the back. I immediately stand up and look behind me to see who it is. It is some random guy grinding on me while his friends observe and cheer him on. I push him off and shoot him an angry face as I walk a few steps to where Tasha is waiting.

"Girl, what in the world was he trying to do!" she yells to me over the music.

"Trying to get a freak dance, but I'm not the one!" I scream back at her.

I touch my forehead and realize I'm sweating more than I want to.

"You want to go to the bathroom real quick?" I yell at Tasha.

She agrees, and we scoot through a crowd of boys, watching a group of girls twerk on the floor.

We go into the bathroom, and it seems every other girl in the party is occupying a stall, hogging mirrors to check their makeup, hair, and body. I look at myself in a corner of a mirror another girl uses and grab a paper towel to wipe the sweat off my face.

I go back outside to wait for Tasha. I look amongst the crowd of dancers and see a girl with a tiny skirt twerking raunchily on a guy who is grabbing and pounding her hips, similar to what the random guy did to me. She is going lower now, and he loves every bit of it. He must have sensed I was watching him because he looks directly at me.

It's Stalker! He catches my eye, immediately lets the girl go, and begins walking over my way. He hasn't texted me since our first kiss, and now he's at this party dancing sexually on some other girl. I roll my eyes as I try to run back into the bathroom to hide from him. Before I can enter, I feel a hand grab and pull me from behind.

"What's up! I didn't know you were going to be here!" he yells into my ear.

He rakes his eyes over my body and then my face.

"Well, you wouldn't know because you didn't text me!" I yell back in his ear.

He starts smiling at me and leans in to respond.

"You want to dance!?" he screams into my ear.

I look up at him and roll my eyes again.

"I'm here with my friend; she'll be out of the bathroom any minute, so you can enjoy dancing with other girls!" I say to him.

Tasha comes out of the bathroom and saves me from my encounter. She comes over to me and examines him while looking back at me. She senses I'm upset and pulls me away from him and into the crowd. I look back, and Stalker stares at me while Tasha drags me.

We continue dancing for the rest of the night, blocking guys who get behind us to get danced on. Tasha sees a friend who lives in her dorm and begins dancing with her. The deejay announces that the next song will be the last one, and we decide that this will be the perfect time to leave before the streets get crowded.

We shimmy through the crowd again when we hear a fight beginning to break out. Tasha, her friend, and I are huddled in the cold, trying to figure out how to get home.

"She and I live on campus, and she has a car, so I can go home with her," Tasha tells me, leaving me out of the equation.

"How am I supposed to get home?" I ask them both.

They look at me as if there's a big question mark on my face.

"Here he comes," Tasha says, pointing behind me.

Stalker walks up behind me with calm eyes.

"Can we talk real fast?" he asks.

I look at him, then quickly glance back at Tasha and her friend, who want to leave me with him.

"Wait, real quick! Don't leave!" I say, walking a few feet away with Stalker.

"Look, I'm sorry about not texting you. I was going to; I didn't know you'd be at this party," he admits.

"It's cool. My friends are waiting for me to leave, so I should be going," I say while looking back at Tasha.

"Do they live at our apartment? If not, you can leave with me since we're going to the same place?" he offers with a smile. He moves a little closer to my shadow.

Dang! I guess it would be wiser to go with him than to have Tasha's friend go out of her way to drop me off. I hate that I must go with him now, but I have no choice.

"I'm going to leave with him since we live in the same place!" I yell at Tasha and her friend.

"Be careful! Text me when you get home! "Tasha yells back as she disappears in the parking lot of cars.

Stalker reacts to her statement with a confused face. He wraps his arm around my waist and directs me to his friend's car.

The car ride home is so cringy. His friend asks me how I knew Stalker, and I just lie that I met him in a class on campus. They look at him and laugh, and then he laughs with his arm still wrapped around me. Maybe if I stare out the window long enough, I'll be home in my apartment. The friend in the passenger seat begins lighting a blunt from his pocket and is passing it around. Stalker takes a hit, then nudges me to take one too.

"I don't smoke," I say to him with a firm voice.

He passes the blunt back to the passenger and stares back into my eyes.

"Okay, okay. Why are you so tense right now?" he asks with a raspy voice.

"I'm just trying to get home," I tell him.

"And you will get home. I won't let anything happen to you," he says. He pulls my waist closer, staring me dead in the eyes.

I stare back at him, and I begin to laugh. He laughs back and releases my waist.

His friends drop us off in front of the leasing office, where I had met Stalker.

"What do you want to do?" he asks while standing over me.

"What do you mean?" I question.

He looks down at me with a blank face.

"Do you want to hang out before we call it a night?" he asks me.

I could hang out with him more since he gave me a ride home—as long as Myesha is home or something.

"You wanna go up to my place?" I offer him.

He starts smiling excitedly as if we're about to do the same thing we did a few nights ago.

We go up the steps and into my apartment, where Myesha sits at the counter in her pajamas.

"Hey, girl!" she says to me.

She looks over at Stalker and then at me with amusement.

"Hello, and who are you?" she asked him.

He leaves my side in a hurry and walks up to her.

"Tomo. I know you; you know my homeboy, Freddie," he tells her.

He looks at her with glossy, big eyes and smiles, as he did when we first met. She begins talking about Freddie, and he sits beside her, examining her face. He is all into her. I walk over and sit behind Myesha as if I were the guest in my place. For a minute, Stalker and Myesha go back and forth, and I just sit there like an intruder in their conversation.

I eventually chime in on a topic they are discussing, and they turn their heads to pay attention. I explain the whole idea, and they listen as if I am giving a speech. Stalker looks more interested in my speech than Myesha. Once I finish, Stalker begins and doesn't stop. Myesha and I give him our undivided attention as he starts chatting and talking about various people.

I'm a bit tipsy and can't understand everything he's saying. However, like Myesha, I just nod my head and continue to let him talk. Two hours go by, and his energy increases as if the night has just started. I excuse myself and go to my room to change out my clothes. When I come back out into the kitchen, he is gone.

"Where did he go?" I ask Myesha in a fatigued tone.

She looks up at me, yawning as she heads for her room.

"He just left because he said you went to your room. He's a little weird," she says as she closes her door.

"Good night," she tells me.

"Good night," I say.

* * *

I wake up the following day in the afternoon with my voice half gone and feeling heavy. I hear my phone buzz from my nightstand.

"Hey, girlie! Let's go eat breakfast today," a text from Tasha reads.

I smile at my screen and slam my head back on my pillow.

It takes me about two hours to officially get out of bed, put on clothes, and get to campus to meet Tasha. Luckily, we were going to one of the dining halls, so I wouldn't have to pay out of pocket for food. I meet Tasha at the corner of the dining hall, and we both look like zombies.

"How did your night end up with old boy?" she asks. Although she usually gets excited, I'll give her a pass today.

"It was okay. Stalker was up all night at my place talking to my roommate and me about a bunch of random things," I tell her.

She looks up at me, then down at her plate.

"That's weird," she says, reiterating the same thing Myesha mentioned.

"Yeah, but I like it. He's different," I say in his defense. "I think I connect with him because he's weird, and people have been calling me weird my entire life. Weird is just another word for different or what I like to call, not basic."

Tasha shrugs her shoulders at my statement and begins recalling the events from the party last night. We gossip about the security guards at the party and critique the deejay on his music selection. I hear my phone buzz on the table about four times and immediately get worried. Who would text me four times if it's not an emergency? I pray it's nothing about a family member or matters regarding back home. I look at my phone, and it's Myesha texting in all caps and exclamation points.

Her texts are unclear, but I skim through them and see something about Stalker from last night.

"Is everything okay?" Tasha asks, observing my face drop.

"It's something with my roommate. I need to get back home," I say to her.

We finish the little food left, and I catch the city bus back to my apartment while Myesha is still there. I walk into the apartment and see her standing in the kitchen with an upset face.

"Girl, come look at this!" she tells me, holding up her phone to my face.

I grab her phone and put it closer to the lens of my glasses to get a better look. It's a DM on social media from Stalker hitting on Myesha. To make it worse, he included a picture of him and his friend and asked her to chill.

My body freezes up. I know this is not what I think it is! He's been chilling with me to have a chance with my roommate this whole time! If he wanted her, why didn't he just pursue her in the first place like every other guy? I let her phone go and look up to her with a straight face. She looks back at me furiously. Myesha has a boyfriend and does not want him to find out about this DM.

"I'm going to see him right now," I say, trembling.

I walk into my room and text him to see if he's home. He says he's home, and I can chill if I want. I agree, and he sends me his apartment number. I'm so mad at him right now that I don't know what to say or do when I see him! All I know is that I will do something that won't end well! I feel like I'm back on the streets at home, and a guy just called me out my name because I didn't want to give him my number. I ball up my fingers and clench them into a fist.

I text him to let him know I am on my way. I also grab my backpack, as I had promised to meet Marcus in the study room later.

I walk over to his place quickly and feel my muscles tightening in my arms and legs. I knock on the door about three times as hard as a cop with a warrant would. He takes five minutes to answer the door and looks at me with a big smile.

"Come on back," he says, gesturing me towards his room.

Despite my frustration, I notice this is my first time in his place. We enter his room, which is tidy and decorated with basketball posters. His shoes line up in a corner, and his school books are stacked on his dresser. The room theme is earthy, with browns and greens throughout his bedsheets and wall paintings. He sits at his desk with his computer open, watching a basketball game, acting as if I'm not even here.

I look at him as if he is on some type of drug. For some reason, I feel a little less angry than on the trip here, but I'm still going to confront him about everything.

"So, what's up with you DMing my roommate and asking her to chill with you?" I ask in a demanding and firm voice.

Stalker turns to the side and squints at me. He then begins smiling and laughing, grabbing his phone from his desk and looking into it.

"I don't know your roommate," he says, with a smirk on his face.

"What?" I ask confusingly. "So, you don't know Myesha, who you met last night and was talking to us for hella hours! Why did you DM her!? If you're trying to talk to her, why even talk to me!?"

I can feel myself starting to get pissed off.

He turns himself in his chair to face me fully.

"Why is there a guy over your place?" he asks. This time, the smirk on his face turns straight.

"What are you even talking about? No guy is at my place, and why are you not answering my questions?" I yell at him again.

He begins to laugh again. "You got a guy over your place," he maintains.

He holds his phone out for me to look at. I'm so furious that I don't want to approach him, but I know I must. I walk over, squinting my eyes through my glasses, and look at his phone screen.

It's a live video story with my roommate Myesha doing dishes in our apartment. Someone is recording her, and she is unaware.

"This is a dude, right?" he asks, looking at me.

I can't believe him right now! First, he lies about being into me just to get to my roommate! Then he lies and says he doesn't even know my roommate while he has some guy do his stalking for him in our apartment! My mind goes blank, and rage takes over. I've never met such a liar in all my years on this earth! My muscles fully tense up, and my adrenaline kicks in.

Without saying a word back to him, I take the palm of my hand, swing it up to his face, and smack him.

His head turns with the smack, then back towards me. I step back from him, preparing for the idea that he may hit me back.

He stares at me as mad as a bull. His eyes get wider and bigger than I've ever seen them before. He stands up quickly. His body is stiff, and he balls up his fists. I can see his veins starting to poke out of his neck and arms.

"Why would you do that!?" he yells at me.

He looms over me, but I don't respond to his question. I brace myself for a hit. He stares at me a little longer, waiting for me to answer. The room goes completely silent. Without warning, he abruptly steps towards me and clinches my neck into the palm of his big hand. He pushes me up against the wall by my throat. I alarmingly scratch at his hands to set me free.

"I...Can't...Breathe!" I struggle to scream.

"Why would you do that!" he screams at me.

In full shock, I pull at his fingers as he squeezes them tightly. I can't manage to get them loose. I can feel my breath getting thin.

"Don't try to fight me!" Stalker tells me.

I throw my arm up and grab his hand that is choking me. I dig my long nails into his flesh and scratch him as hard as I can.

When I release his arm, he drops me onto the ground,

leaving me gasping for air. My vision is blurred, and my head feels dizzy.

When my sight gets back to normal, I look up at him.

The scratch is long and bloody. He doesn't make a sound. He stares down at his wounded arm and then looks down at me.

I don't move from my position on the ground. I'm afraid that if I do, he might do something drastic. We stay in place, staring each other in the eyes.

He lunges for my backpack and quickly begins heading for the front door to throw it outside.

I immediately go after him.

"Tomo! Why are you doing this? I barely hit you at all!" I cry at him.

I jump in front of the door to block him from opening it.

His eyes are those of a demon. I've only seen these eyes in my father. His grip on my bag is so tight that he might rip it open. His nostrils are flaring out of control. All I can think about is me going to jail or dying tonight.

He forcefully shoves through me, trying to open the door. I feel myself almost blackout. I start wrestling him with all my muscles. Stalker pushes up against me using all his strength and manages to get the door open a little less than halfway. I can feel my grip against him loosening. I use whatever extra strength my adrenaline allows me to have and push up against him harder. I slam the door shut and snatch my bag out of his hand.

He stands back, breathing heavily, staring at me in anger but in shock at my strength.

"You don't know where I'm from! I will kill you and go to jail!" I yell at him as I carefully bend over to pick up my bag.

"Are you going to behave!?" he screams at me.

"Am I going to do what!? I'm not your child!" I retort.

I look at him in disgust. Then, I turn around, yank the door to his apartment open, and sprint out.

Chapter Six

THE STUDY ROOM

I can feel tears coming down my face out of anger. My phone buzzes, and it's a text from Marcus.

"Hey, DJ! We're in the big study room waiting on you," it reads.

If I cancel on them and go home, my anger and thoughts will overtake me and push me to do something I regret. Staring at my phone screen, I slowly text, "I'm on my way."

With my backpack hanging off one shoulder, I take a few deep breaths to calm myself and smile before I walk into the room. I can hear Marcus and Alonzo's laughter, which gives me the courage to turn the corner and push the door open.

"Hey! What's up, DJ!" Marcus screams with excitement.

His face looks so vibrant and lights up when he sees me. He stands up and holds his arms out for me to come and embrace them. Alonzo laughs at Marcus and smiles at me from the side. I drop my bag and walk into Marcus for a hug. I need this more than he knows. I grip his body, and he is warm. I feel my anger go away, and happiness fills my body for a second. We release each other, and his smile is still on his face. He squints and looks at me. I smile back at him.

"You can sit anywhere you want," he tells me, pointing to every seat in the house.

"How about I just sit in the middle of you guys? That way, we can bounce ideas about how we will take over this school," I say jokingly.

They look at me, and we all burst out laughing.

"Sounds like a good plan!" Alonzo says as he takes out his laptop from his bag.

"Unfortunately, Alonzo and I have some algorithm homework we have to do. What about you?" Marcus asks me.

I look down at my backpack and can only think about Stalker choking me.

"Some Biology homework for my lab," I lie.

"Wow! I have some knowledge of biology, so if you need help, I'm here," Marcus responds.

I reach into my bag, grab my laptop, and notice a massive dent on its side. Alonzo holds his water bottle and stands up from his seat.

"I'll be right back. About to fill up my bottle at the water fountain," he says, smiling at both Marcus and me.

"Gotta get them proper nutrients to do them algorithms!" I joke with him.

They both laugh, and he nods at my joke as he goes to the door.

Once Alonzo leaves, I look over at Marcus while he is working. His eyes are smiling, and he seems to focus on his screen, but I can tell he is not doing any work.

"Looking real busy over there!" I joke with him.

He laughs and gives me his full attention. "DJ with the jokes!

I didn't know you were this funny," he says while getting out a pen.

"You say it like it's a bad thing or something. Is it?" I say with a straight face. My eyes begin to water.

I quickly stare down at my computer screen and wipe the tears.

"No, it's not a bad thing! Is everything okay?" Marcus asks me.

He rolls his chair away from his computer to my seat. His face has now turned concerned.

I don't respond to his question.

"You know you can tell me anything. I'm not here to judge. If something is going on, we can talk about it. I want to help," he encourages me.

"Do you know a guy named Tomo that lives here?" I ask him, looking up from my computer.

"Yes, I do! He lives right next door to me." Marcus says.

I jump out of my seat.

"You're lying! This lunatic is your neighbor!?" I say out loud.

Marcus's eyes widen. I can tell he is startled by my outburst. How can Stalker and Marcus even live next to each other? One is a gentleman, kind and thoughtful, and the other is an abusive, creepy liar.

"Hey, hey, calm down! I don't know him like that, but I've met him, and he seems pretty cool. How do you know him?" he asks me with a confused tone.

He waves at me to sit down and puts on his investigator's face.

I return to my seat and choose the facts I want to tell. There's no way I'm going to tell him what we did the first night we hung out or that he choked me out just now. I tell him briefly that I met him in front of the leasing office, that he hung out with my roommate and me, and that he just tried to throw my things out the door.

Marcus's face drops mid-story and stays that way until the end. His eyes are focused, and he is in disbelief in the actions I described of Stalker—if only he knew the whole truth.

"Wow, DJ, that's a lot! Do you mean to tell me he was trying to hit on you, then turned around and tried to get your roommate, too? Then you hit him for his behavior, and he tried to throw your things out!?" he asks in a high-pitched voice.

I look at him with an "I can't make this up" expression and nod at his summary.

"Wow! That is crazy!" he says.

Marcus sees Alonzo approaching the door to the study room.

"Alonzo told me he could only study for about an hour, so when he leaves, let's continue this conversation," Marcus says, smiling, and then he rubs my shoulder and tells me everything will be okay.

Alonzo walks back through the door. "I heard somebody yelling. Is homework making one of y'all that mad!" he teases.

We begin laughing out loud.

"DJ just got a little carried away with this biology homework; something about cells drives her crazy!" Marcus explains, with a crazy look on his face.

I fold up a sheet of paper and get up to hit him with it. He flinches as he rolls his chair away from me.

Alonzo begins laughing, and I come after him next with the paper. They both start running from me as I chase them around the table.

After the paper fight, we return to our seats to work but never do. We joke, laugh, and talk the entire night. After around two hours, Alonzo tells us he has to leave the study room, but it's clear to us that this will be the place that marks our friendship. Once Alonzo closes the door to the study room, the world revolves around Marcus and I. We put away our school things, roll our chairs in front of each other, and begin expressing our feelings about the world and everyone in it. I tell him more about Stalker and am relieved that I can talk to someone about it. He listens to me and gives me advice. He tells me I'm strong and to never allow Stalker to treat me like that. He encourages me and compliments me.

I'm beginning to love the study room already.

* * *

The next couple of months go by really fast. It feels like I'm having the best time of my life! Marcus sends me good morning texts, and we text throughout the day now. I go to campus, and Tasha and I follow the same routine. Then, I head back to the apartment to meet Marcus and Alonzo in the study room.

I never do any work when I'm with these two. The last time, Alonzo showed Marcus and me how to do this funny dance with a catchy but stupid song. His dancing was so amusing that I got up and copied his movements. Marcus rooted for me as I moved step by step until I got it right. After I got it down, I motioned Marcus to get up and try the dance. He hesitated but then got up to do it. Alonzo and I mocked him as he tried to get the footwork. He cursed at us, and then we all danced together. We look like a small fraternity that only picks a few members to join.

This is where I spend the majority of my time now. I talk and hang out with Marcus every day, all day. I call him the male version of myself and my best friend. One day, we were hanging out in the study room, talking about being mad at someone and how to release anger. Marcus explained that we shouldn't let anyone have that much power over us where they can make us act out. He stated that he's the best at not getting out of character.

That's when I told him he was the best at being my best friend. His eyes got glossy, and he told me to hug him. I happily embraced him, and we hugged for a long time. I told him he was the only one who'd been here for me and the only one I could talk to. He told me I was a joy to be around, and my happiness made him happy.

The next day, Marcus and I meet in the morning to take the 9:00 a.m. shuttle bus to campus. We don't have class until noon, but I found this cool place to hang out until one of us has to leave. It's a low-key study room on campus with a built-in market, which means unlimited snacks! We get on the shuttle and pick a seat close to the back of the bus.

"You sure we're allowed to study in this place you found?" Marcus questions me.

I put down my bag and look over at his confused face.

"Yes! Tasha and I found this place one week ago, and it's a good spot to chill." I tell him.

More kids are getting on the shuttle bus, and we realize this may be a packed route. I look up and see Stalker getting on the bus and heading toward the back row. I immediately look down, trying not to make eye contact. I don't know how I feel about him right now.

Stalker catches eyes with Marcus and stops at our seat.

"What's up man, what's going on!?" Stalker asks Marcus.

I look up, but he doesn't even look in my direction.

"Cool, man, I'm chilling!" Marcus says back.

They give each other a dap, and Stalker continues to walk to the back of the shuttle.

I look over at Marcus with wide eyes, and my mouth drops.

"What's up, DJ? You cool?" he asks me.

"So he saw you but acted like he didn't see me? Do I look invisible to you?" I ask Marcus.

He looks back at Stalker, then looks back at me.

"I mean, maybe he didn't see you? Have y'all spoken since the fight?" Marcus questions.

"No, but that doesn't give him a reason to act like I don't exist," I say back.

Marcus looks at me as if I'm crazy, but that's because he doesn't know everything. He doesn't know that I've kissed and touched his neighbor, let alone the things his neighbor has done to me.

"Anyway, we can grab some snacks when we get there!" I roar as I hit Marcus on the shoulder.

He squints his eyes at me and rubs the spot on his shoulder I just hit.

"Okay, cool," he says to me.

"I'm sorry! Did I hit you too hard? Let me rub it for you," I tell Marcus as I begin massaging his shoulder.

He looks at me with the most confused face in the world. "I'm good. It's cool," he says, leaning back in his seat.

"Okay! I'm still thinking about you tryna get that dance down! It was so funny!" I say as I begin laughing out loud.

Marcus looks me up and down and looks back at Stalker.

The shuttle finally arrives at campus, and Marcus and I get off the bus and begin walking toward the study room with the market.

"Hold up real quick!" Marcus shouts to me as I lead the way.

"What's up!" I say back.

"I saw what you did on the bus back there," Marcus tells me.

I stop walking and amble a few feet back to where he's standing.

"What do you mean?" I ask him.

"You were flirting with me on the bus so Tomo can see," he tells me.

I look up at the sky and then back down at him.

"No! I wasn't doing that! I don't care about him," I lie to Marcus.

Marcus looks up and chuckles.

"Yes, you were! I know what flirting looks like, and I saw your whole mood change as soon as he walked up," he informs me.

Could he tell that my mood changes around him?

"Of course, I'm still mad about the fight! But I wasn't trying to use you for anything," I lie to him again.

Marcus looks me dead in my eyes.

"Ok. If you say you weren't," he says.

He grips his backpack and begins walking toward the path of the study room. I stand there for a few moments as I figure out how the rest of the day will go before I follow behind him.

I had told Marcus everything about me except for the intimate and abusive things that happened with Stalker. As we walk, I wonder how well Marcus and Stalker know each other. He said he only met him once, but their encounter on the bus shows they know each other more than I think. Maybe Stalker is both of our secrets?

We get to the study room, and Marcus agrees to put our things down while I grab the snacks from the market. I wonder what he thinks the whole time I'm shopping for snacks. I don't want to trouble our friendship with lies. What if he is lying to me as well? I go to the table, and Marcus has his laptop out already. He doesn't look up at me.

"I got the snacks! I got your favorite bag of chips!" I say, handing him the bag.

"Thanks," he says, motioning for me to put them on the table.

We sit in silence for a few moments.

"Are you mad at me about the whole bus thing?" I come out and ask.

He looks up from his computer. "I'm not mad; I just think it's things you're not telling me," he admits.

"Like what!" I ask him.

"I don't know, but y'all need to talk it out because I could sense tension between you," he tells me.

"I guess," I say back to him.

Marcus is right. I am lying.

I have seen Stalker after the fight.

Chapter Seven:
THE BACK AND FORTH

The week after the fight, I saw Stalker on the morning shuttle on my way to campus. He is usually not on the bus, but he was this time. I made eye contact with him and sat as far away from his seat as possible. Once the bus started moving, he got up from his seat and found me in mine.

"Can we talk?" he asked me.

"I guess I have no choice. You just bum-rushed my seat!" I said in frustration.

"Let's just dead the other night. My homie was trying to talk to your roommate, so what's the problem?" he asked.

I looked at him like a madman. He didn't even mention the fight.

"You are my problem!" I said.

I pushed myself as close to the window as possible and began staring out the window, hoping he'd get the hint and go away.

"I see how you're trying to do me. Look, you have a cute smile, and you're thick. You're not fine or anything," he said to me.

"What the fuck are you talking about!? Is this your way of hitting on me because you've already done that!" I yelled at him.

The other few students on the bus began to look back at us.

"I'm not trying to hit on you. I would hit on a chick that's way badder," he said.

"Leave me the fuck alone!" I screamed at him.

This time, he removed himself from my seat and away from my sight.

My phone buzzed in my hand, and I looked to see who it was. It was Stalker texting me.

"Just meet me at my place tonight to talk this out," it read.

I ignored the message. The shuttle stopped on campus, and I gathered my things and quickly rose from my seat. Looking ahead in the aisle, I saw Stalker staring at me. He did this for a moment before he left the bus. I shook my head and allowed a minute to pass before I left the bus.

My first class went as usual, and Tasha and I went to a dining hall. She had met this guy at her job and couldn't wait to tell me all the details. For the first time, I was interested in her gossip— anything that would keep me distracted and away from mine.

"This dude is so fine! And I think he is a part of one of those fraternities!" she said with excitement.

I looked up at her and then looked down at my plate.

"He was flirting with me and asking me what class I was in. I told him I was a freshman, and he said, 'See, I can't even mess with you if you're a freshman,'" she went on.

"So, he trying to tell you that fraternity boys don't mess with freshmen! They do this all the time!" I told her.

"I know girl! So, have you seen Stalker since the fight?" she asked me.

I thought her gossip was going to last the whole lunch. I never told her about him choking me.

'No, and I hope it stays that way," I replied.

She accepted my answer, and we continued eating.

After my day on campus, I headed back to my apartment. Since the morning text, Stalker texted me again, asking if I was coming to his place. After what he's said and done to me, I shouldn't do anything but call the cops on him, but something in the back of my mind told me to go to finish this once and for all. Like an idiot, I decided to go.

His place remained the same since I last visited. He sat on his bed while I sat in a chair in the corner of his room. He stared at me, and I quickly glanced over at him.

"Come here," he directed me.

"Why should I?" I asked him.

" Because I want to tell you something," came his reply.

"Why can't you just tell me right now?" I asked.

He got up from his spot on the bed and stood in front of me. My heart began to race. I looked up at him, and he grabbed my hands and put them in his. He pulled me up from the chair, staring at my lips. Then he pulled me towards him until we flopped onto the bed, with me on top of him.

"Look," I said with my hands on his chest.

He slid his hands on top of my thighs and began squeezing and rubbing me.

"We don't have to talk," he whispered to me.

He pushed my body forward and leaned in for a kiss.

I jerked my face away from his, but he gently touched my chin and slowly directed it toward his face. His eyes never leave mine.

"Why are we doing this?" I asked softly.

He paused, chuckled a little, and then smiled.

"Because we want to," he replied.

We began kissing and touching each other all over.

He flipped me over and got in between my legs. He lifted my shirt and bra and started kissing and caressing my breasts.

I started breathing deeply at the sense of his touch. It is firm but gentle. He slid one hand down my thigh and began rubbing. I began lifting my legs as he slowly grinded in between them. I moaned softly as I felt him getting hard. He likes it when I do this. He quietly moaned, too, humping me to a fast rhythm. Though we were humping, we were still fully clothed.

Once he stopped, I looked up at his face, and he smiled and glared at the ceiling. I reached for his face, rubbing his chin and combing his hair with my hand. He looked down and followed my hand movement with his eyes. We said nothing to each other. He softly began to rub my hips, then my back.

"What do you want from me?" I asked him with a soft voice.

He laughed. "Is this your favorite question to ask me? You do this all the time."

"Because I don't know what we are doing? What do you want?" I asked him again.

I've noticed that he never seems to answer anything I ask him or address the horrible things he's done and said to me. He just ignores the question and says what he wants. This was the second time clothes burning, and he hadn't even apologized for the fight.

"Let me know if you are rocking with me. Are you?" he asked me. He turned me into his arms so my face was before him.

"What are you talking about?" I asked.

"Put my hands on your body so I know you are rocking with me," he directed me.

I laughed out loud.

He frowned at me and released me from his arms.

"Wait, wait, okay, okay! If you're asking me If I like you, then maybe, I guess," I said to him.

He smiled, grabbed me, and put me back in his arms. Then he began laughing.

"So you like the kid, huh?" he joked.

I gave him a mini slap on his face, and he bit my hand playfully.

He laughed at my reaction and leaned in to kiss me.

The next day on campus, Tasha and I decided to hang out in the student center and study during the day. I don't know why we even lied to ourselves about studying, knowing that we would talk the whole time. The center was busy with students getting ready for homecoming, the most significant time of the year in college other than graduation. People were handing out flyers about why they should be on the royal homecoming court. Fraternities and Sororities were strolling through students promoting their annual step show, and the football team was hanging in the corner, lingering in their popularity.

"Girl, I ordered food, and it's ready! I'm about to get it, and then we can start studying!" Tasha told me.

"Okay! Hurry back because this biology test is in a few days!" I reminded her.

I looked around the room at all the commotion, and a girl running for homecoming queen caught my eye.

"Hi! Vote for me for homecoming queen this year!" she said, handing me her flyer.

"Sure!" I said, smiling as I took the flyer from her hand.

I watched her leave the table and hug a group of guys. They all wore flashy clothes and had girls walking on each side. I noticed that Stalker was in this group. He hugged the girl tightly, smiled, and took her flyer. She smiled widely back at him and rubbed his arm before she left. Stalker's eyes met mine from across the room, and he looked away quickly. His group was walking near my table. I smiled as I braced myself to greet him, but as soon as his group passed my table, he looked straight ahead and began talking to the girl next to him.

Tasha walked back to the table.

"Hey, girl! Why does your face look like that?" she asked me.

"I know he saw me right here!" I yelled out loud.

Tasha put her lunch on the table and looked me up and down.

"Who you talking about!?" she asked.

"Stalker! He made eye contact with me and walked right past me!" I told her.

I glanced back at him and his friends. They were sitting near popular fraternity brothers, laughing and talking to girls who flocked to their table.

"Oh, I see what game he is playing! He wants to act like he doesn't know me, but last night, he was… never mind!" I stopped myself.

Tasha's eyes got wide, and she began to turn red.

"Last night he what?!" she questioned a little loudly.

"Huh! I wasn't even going to tell you!" I said back.

She moved her seat close to mine.

"Tell me what! I thought you said you wouldn't speak to him again, especially after the fight!" she demanded.

"I wasn't! But then he hit me up like come over, let's talk this out, and then when I went over there, we ended up doing no talking and all action," I told her.

"Wait! Y'all had sex!" she screamed out.

I looked around the neighboring tables to see if anyone heard her.

"Would you shut up! And No! We didn't have sex, but we got intimate," I hissed, my voice barely louder than a whisper.

I could tell she was just eating all of this up.

"You need to tell me everything!" she demanded.

"Huh!" I huffed.

I looked around the area to ensure no one was close enough to hear, and then I told her every last detail of the night before. I didn't tell her about the first night or the choking. I had decided to keep that a secret. As I talked, Tasha looked like she might explode from all these juicy details.

"And you said he looked at you and walked right past you?" she questioned when I was done.

She looked at the table where he sat with his friends and saw him put his arm around a girl.

"Girl, Look over there! He is playing you! He got hoes, and he's up here chilling with you in private and ignoring you in public!" she told me.

I looked over at him, and Tasha was right. I couldn't believe I let him play me like this! I knew this virgin thing was a lie! It was he who wanted Myesha, not his friend. He lied to me once, and he lied to me again. But why me? Why mess with me if you don't want to? I know I'm not the 'show off to your friends' type of girl! I don't fit his image. He is more popular than I thought he was. When we met, I assumed he was a low-key guy.

After an hour or so of Tasha and I discussing everything but homework, we finally got to studying for our biology exam. The sun began to set, and I realized the last shuttle home would be in 15 minutes.

"Huh! I have to go to get this shuttle home," I informed her.

"That's cool! We can just start fresh tomorrow!" she said.

I quickly packed up my things and ran out of the student center to the bus stop three minutes away. When I got to the stop, Stalker was talking with a friend. I stood in the shadows, waiting for the shuttle to come. At this point, I wanted to forget I even met him. The shuttle arrived, and he and his friend got on the bus. I let a couple of other kids get in front of me before I got on.

I walked up the steps, and Stalker and I made eye contact again. He was looking directly at me. I immediately sat in the seat directly behind the driver. Stalker has some nerve. The shuttle took off, and I could only think about the previous night. I thought we were moving forward from the complications of our friendship, but I was dead wrong. The bus driver saw my face in her rearview mirror and made small talk with me. She is a hilarious lady, and at one point, the only voices you could hear on the bus were ours.

We pulled up at the apartment, and the bus driver and I continued to talk as the other kids got off the bus. I felt a shadow standing over me, and I knew it was Stalker behind me. I heard his voice as he began to chime in our conversation. I told the driver bye and gathered my things to get off the bus. Stalker followed right behind me. Once the bus drove off, he reached for my hand and pulled me back towards him.

"No, no, no! You don't get to do that," I told him with a straight face.

He smiled as he let go of my hand.

"What did I do now?" he asked.

"It's not what you did. It's what you didn't do!" I yelled at him.

"Okay. What didn't I do?" he asked me.

Is this dude serious right now?

"You saw me walking with your clique in the student center today, and you didn't say anything to me. I can't even get a hello, huh!?" I asked.

He laughed and motioned me to walk with him.

"I did not see you today," he said.

I stopped walking and looked him dead in his eyes. Smacking him again sounded good right now.

"So you didn't make eye contact with me while walking with your friends, and that girl came up to you to give you her homecoming flyer!?" I asked him.

He looked up with a confused expression.

"'No, I didn't. Are you stalking me or something?" he questioned.

I began to laugh out loud.

"You should be the last person calling someone a stalker! Are you trying to call me crazy? I know we made eye contact!" I insisted.

"Well, I'm telling you we didn't, and I didn't see you. What's up with you?" he asked, stopping to look at me face to face.

"I'm not crazy, but you gone make me go there with you. I know you looked at me," I maintained.

"How do you know?" he asked, taking his backpack off one of his shoulders.

"Because I know how you look at me," I said.

He laughed and began walking again.

"And you're such a liar! You got all these hoes, and you probably got a girlfriend!" I said, putting all the pieces of the puzzle together.

He laughed again and turned to face me.

"No. I don't have a girlfriend—I told you that already—and I don't have hoes. If anything, you are my hoe," he stated.

I dropped my bag on the ground and ran up into his face.

"I'm your what!" I screamed.

I ball my fist up, ready to hit him with a sucker punch this time, just like I do to the guys back at home.

"Just chill, alright!" he told me.

I stood there in his face a bit longer, daring him to call me out my name again. He didn't try the dare, and I walked back to get my bag off the ground.

"Watch yourself because I'm so close to catching a case with you! You got me fucked up!" I yelled at him.

I gave him an aggressive stare, then power walked up the steps to my apartment.

The following two weeks passed, and I saw Stalker multiple times on campus from my classes. Most days, we made eye contact but never spoke. He mostly walked with a girl or one of his friends, who would stare me down as I walked past. I assumed he was telling his friends crazy things about me, like how I'm his hoe or how we like bruising each other in private.

One day, I went to a women's empowerment gathering on campus and met this girl who recognized me by face. She looked at me from across the room and walked up to me with her mouth wide open.

"Do you happen to be DJ by any chance?" she asked me.

I took a sip of the free drinks the event was offering and squinted at her face to see if I recognized her.

"Why yes! That is me. Have we met before?" I said.

She looked around us to ensure no one else was standing close enough to hear what she was about to say, and then she moved closer to me.

"No. I haven't, but I've heard your name in conversations with a couple of guy friends, and they say many interesting things," she replied.

My heart dropped to my stomach.

"What kind of things are you hearing?" I asked her with a straight face.

"You are smashing one of the guys in the AO, aren't you?"

she asked me. Her enormous eyes looked into my eyes for the answer.

"No! I'm not having sex with any guy at this school!" I said aloud.

Some of the other women in the room began looking our way.

"Well, one of the guys in the African Organization has been telling some juicy stories about you. It's cool though, girl, he's fine!" she told me, smiling.

She walked away and went over to hug another girl by the door.

I then knew for sure that Stalker was talking trash about me! How did she know how I looked? The stares his friends gave me every time they see me have to mean something! What makes it even worse is that we don't have the same friend circle, so his friends have no choice but to believe the crazy things he says about me. I can't defend myself. I put down my drink and left the event upset and sad.

The end of the week came, and Homecoming finally arrived! Tasha, a couple of new friends, and I made plans to pre-game and leave as a big group for the festivities! I didn't tell Tasha, but Myesha and I had been drinking since we woke up. Myesha felt I was not as energetic as usual, and I told her I was going through a lot emotionally. She told me she'd been there and asked if I wanted to get tipsy with her at a day party she was invited to, and I took her offer. I just wanted to get so fucked up that I wouldn't remember anything! I wanted to find a fine-ass guy to twerk on and live my best life carefree! Mostly, I wanted to forget about everything going on with Stalker.

"Girl, are you okay? You seem like you're already geeked!"
Tasha said to me.

We were at my friend's house getting ready in the bathroom.
I was screaming to the rap music and twerking so fast that my
boobs were beginning to pop out the top of my dress.

"Yass! I'm good, I just want to get so fucked up and find
me a fine tenderoni! You know what I'm saying!" I screamed.

I smiled and looked at Tasha with baby eyes. She laughed
and slapped my thigh while I continued to twerk.

"I like your energy! We gone have fun tonight!" she yelled.

When our other friends heard us turning up, they ran into
the bathroom and began twerking with me in the mirror.

We drank bottle after bottle until we all felt numb. It was
cold outside, but we all felt warm, and I began talking too
much—something I do when I'm drunk.

"I'm so ready to go to this party! Fuck Stalker and his
friends!" I yelled out to Tasha.

"Hahaha! Yes, Girl! Fuck him!" she responded.

We got to the party, and it was like any other party: weed
smoke, overcrowding, blasting music, and a few OK dudes. I let
the music take over my body as I began rolling my hips. All the
girls in our group held hands as we maneuvered through the
crowd until we found a space big enough to fit all of us. Once
we got there, we all began twerking on each other, grabbing
thighs, slapping butts, and recording our actions. I was having
too much fun! I saw a sexy, muscular guy standing by me. He
looked at me up and down and licked his lips.

"You like something you see!" I yelled at him over the loud
music.

He stared down at my waist and walked over behind me. Then, he slid his hands on my lower back and talked in my ear.

"Yes, I do! You look fine as hell tonight! Can I get a dance, beautiful?" he asked me.

I laughed and started to bend down while rolling my hips against his pants. He grabbed my waist as I began to twerk on him real fast in a circular motion. My friends saw me and surrounded us in a circle. They cheered me on, and I began doing tricks I only do in my bathroom mirror. They look shocked, to say the least. I stopped and looked at the guy behind me; his face was lit up! His eyes and mouth were smiling at me continuously. He grabbed my hands and pulled me into him.

"You need to take my number! You are the bomb, baby girl!" he told me.

I laughed at his statement, took my phone out of my purse, and handed it to him. He entered his number and told me to text him as soon as possible! He rubbed his hands on my lower back and walked away, smiling.

"Girl! I know you had ass, but I didn't know you could do all that!" my other friend squealed.

"Well, you know! Everybody can't know everything!" I laughed.

We all began dancing again to the next song coming on.

I heard my phone buzz about five times, and I assumed it was the guy I just gave the best dance of the night. I looked at my phone, and it was Stalker.

His messages read, "Hey, wassup! Where are you at? Are you at that party? You should come over after. I miss you."

I continued to look down at the messages. I was no longer dancing, and my face was straight. I didn't know what to do. Tasha noticed me standing still and came over.

"Hey, girl! What's going on!?" she yelled at me over the music.

I hurriedly put my phone away.

"Nothing! I was just looking at something stupid!" I yelled back to her.

She grabbed my hands and pulled me over to where our friend group was dancing and having the time of their lives. She let me go, bent down, and began twerking on my hips. I smiled and cheered her on.

Once the party was over, all our friends said goodbye and agreed to make it a mission for us to all go out again. Tasha and I hugged each other, and she told me we could go to the dining hall tomorrow for breakfast if I wanted. I took her offer, and one of my other friends, who didn't feel drunk anymore, drove me home. Once she dropped me off at the apartment, I immediately took out my phone and scrolled to the messages from Stalker. A part of me hates his guts for the disrespectful way he treats me. The other part of me missed his goofy, sexual side.

"Okay. I'll be there in 10," I texted back to him.

Without even a second passing, he texted me back: "Cool. I'll leave the door open."

I went back to my apartment, still drunk and hardly able to function. I slipped out of my dress, put on a crop top and short shorts, and headed to his place. I opened the door to his apartment, and it was dark. His other roommates didn't seem to be home. Out of nowhere, I felt a hand grab mine and pull me close.

"I'm right here," he said in a deep, slow voice.

I giggled and followed the hand to where it guided me.

His room was dark. The only light came from the TV, and the volume was set to low. I began talking about my night at the club in a drunk and chopped voice.

"I had... so much fun... tonight!" I said.

"You did," he responded.

He held my waist as he closed the door behind me. He only had a pair of boxers on. As soon as he closed the door, he pushed me up against the wall and began to make out with me hard. He took one hand off my waist and put it underneath my chin as he started sticking his tongue down my throat. I threw my arms around his neck and thrust my tongue into his mouth. He grabbed my thighs and motioned me toward the bed. I took off my shirt mid-way, and he took me and pinned me to the bed. He quickly slid in between my legs and began sucking and kissing me on my neck.

He moved his hands down to the hole of his boxers and pulled out his flesh fully erected. He began stroking me but did not pull down my shorts. Since my shorts were thin, I could feel him now more than at any other time. He flipped me over and stroked me from the backside. It felt like we were having sex this time.

Once he stopped, he leaned over me to where my face was smashed into his pillow and slid his tongue down my throat. I giggled and tangled up my tongue with his. He got up from on top of me and went into the bathroom to clean off. He exited the bathroom, wrapped his body around mine, and smiled. He took my hands in his and began massaging my fingers.

"I swear. When we do have sex, I'mma sleep in it," he said to me.

I turned my head to stare into his eyes.

"Why don't we?" I questioned him.

He looks down into my eyes and begins to laugh.

"Because you don't want to have sex," he replied.

"I don't want to have sex? You know I'm not a virgin, right?" I said.

"Yeah, you told me that, but you are scared to have sex with me," he responded.

I unwrapped myself from his body and sat on top of him with my legs spread open around his waist.

"I'm not afraid to have sex, but I think you are," I told him.

He grabbed my waist. "I'm not afraid. I can tell you are. We can just do it when you're ready."

I looked down at him and smiled, and he smiled back.

"Okay," I agreed.

I didn't know what he was talking about, but I was starting to think he was actually a virgin and was afraid to initiate sex, probably because he didn't know how. Unfortunately for him, I don't know how to initiate sex either. The few guys I have been with have always done it, so it's never something I had to worry about doing. At that moment, I forgot everything he had done to me.

"You said you missed me. What do you miss?" I asked him.

He looked into my soul and smirked.

"I miss them lips, that ass, and what we do. You not talking to other dudes, are you?" he asked me.

I laughed out loud at his question.

"That's none of your business if you're not my man," I responded.

He looked over at the clock, and it was almost 4 a.m.

"You should probably get home, and I should probably get some sleep for work tomorrow morning," he said to me.

"Oh, you just got what you wanted, and now you're kicking me out?" I asked him with a straight face.

"No, it's just late, and I have to be somewhere tomorrow. You can spend the night anytime you want. Just let me know," he informed me.

He walked me to the front door of his apartment. We made out for about two minutes before I told him goodbye and walked back to my apartment building alone.

I woke up feeling like I was in love the following day. I couldn't help but smile when I thought about the night before. I got a text from Tasha asking me to go to breakfast with her. I felt bad from all the drinking from yesterday, but the emotions I felt from last night with Stalker made me numb to the feeling. Looking like a hot mess, I quickly showered, slipped on some baggy sweatpants and a T-shirt, and headed to the bus stop to meet Tasha on campus. We met at our favorite dining hall and filled our plates.

"Girl! Last night was so much fun! Did you text that guy

from last night!" she asked, glancing at me.

I began smiling and laughing at the thought of Stalker.

"He texted you!" she screamed.

"Yeah, he did!" I lied.

"That dude was fine, and he was feeling you. Maybe you'll get some!" she told me, looking down at my thighs.

"What! Girl, I don't need some of anything!" I said back.

Tasha was right! I hadn't had sex since high school, and the clothes burning with Stalker was making me sexually frustrated! I would love to get some and stop all the playing around, but I want it to be with Stalker. I'd never wanted to have sex with a guy as bad as I wanted to have sex with Stalker at this point. The physical chemistry between us was so much that it was exhausting.

The following week started, and I was feeling better emotionally. On my way to class, I saw Stalker and waited for him to pass my way so I could talk to him and maybe even hug him like the other girls do. He glanced at me and continued walking without acknowledging me. My face melted, and my eyes got glossy. What did I do to deserve this treatment?

Chapter Eight:
THE ONE NIGHT STAND

At this point, I can't explain what I'm feeling. I lied to Marcus about seeing Stalker after the fight. I don't think he will trust what I say anymore. Even though I haven't admitted it, I know he knows. He knows my soul. He knows my heart. He just knows. We haven't hung out since the flirting issue on the bus, and Stalker is ignoring me for whatever reason.

I am back to being alone like I was at the beginning of the school year. I texted Tasha to hang out, but she had a family emergency back home and had to leave during the week. For the first time, I have to find food on my own after class. I walk alone. I feel alone. I am alone. For the next couple of days, I stayed cooped up in my room after I came home from campus. I don't send texts; no one has sent anything to me. I realize how much time I've been giving Marcus and Stalker. Without them, I had no other friends I spent time with daily. I have no affiliations with organizations that interest me, and the school year is almost over. My grades went from A's to B's, and C's not because I'm not smart, but because I spend more time in study rooms goofing off than actually studying for tests.

My phone buzzes, and I quickly go and see who it is. Maybe it's Marcus! Perhaps he's ready to forgive me and begin hanging out with me again! I look down and see a message from that fine guy from the party.

The message reads, "Hey beautiful! Long time no see! You doing anything tonight?"

I instantly begin to smile. I forgot all about dude! He was fine!

"Hey, buddy! I'm not doing anything. What do you want to do?" I respond.

I'm lying in bed, snuggled in my covers with my hair in a messy updo. It is a rainy, gloomy day, and the only light shining in my room is a dim desk lamp that needs a new bulb.

"We can just chill! I live in the apartments across the street from the grocery store. Where do you live?" his message reads.

"Wait, I live in the apartments across from the grocery store too!" I replied.

I never saw this guy on the shuttle bus, in the study room, or anywhere else this year. Maybe I was so busy with two other guys that I wasn't paying attention to any other guys who lived here. He gives me his apartment number, and I tell him I'll see him in a few.

I remove the covers from on top of me and jump up to stare at myself in the mirror.

"Okay! Even though he is fine, you will not have sex with him. That's for Stalker once he gets his act right!" I say to myself out loud in the mirror.

The school year is almost over, and all I've done was get teased by a dick print the entire time here. I know Stalker and I aren't talking, but he's the only guy I've been intimate with since the beginning, and because of his lies, everyone already thinks we smashed anyway. I know this is not an excuse, but he is the only one who knows how to deal with my body and touch me the way I like.

I keep on my same clothes and brush my hair down neatly before I head out the door. I figure if I don't dress up or anything, I won't feel the urge to have sex. I get to the guy's place, and he smiles wide as soon as he opens the door. He is tall and looks like he just got out of the shower.

"Hey, beautiful! Come inside," he says, motioning me to enter.

I enter his apartment and head for the couch.

"That night was crazy! I wasn't even feeling the party for real until I saw you," he says to me, smirking.

He sits next to me and offers to play some music.

"You got any good suggestions?" he asks me.

I grab his game controller connected to his TV and type in a low-key song I love to listen to. The song begins to play, and he instantly begins bobbing his head to the tempo.

"When it comes to music, I'm the right one to ask. My whole playlist is fire!" I tell him.

He laughs and begins to dance, reminding me of the silly dance Alonzo taught Marcus and me. I get up and start doing the same dance. He begins rooting me on and watching me from behind. We laugh and fall onto the couch.

"I like you. You're cool and have a different vibe than most girls," he tells me.

"A different vibe? I guess I know what you mean," I say to him.

"Let's go into the room. I'll let you pick the movie," he tells me, getting up and going into his room.

I'm starting to get nervous. I don't want to go into his room right now. I look at his room and look at the front door.

"You coming in?" he asks me from inside his room.

"Yeah, I'm coming," I say to him, looking at the front door.

I get up and slowly walk into his room. The lights are off besides the light coming from the TV. He is already in bed with the covers pulled over him. I sit at the edge of the bed.

"You know you can get a little closer than that," he says, looking at me with a grin.

I glance over at him and force out a smile.

"Make yourself comfortable. You can take your jacket off, too," he explains to me.

To avoid speaking, I moved closer to him, removed my jacket, and placed it on the arm of his headboard.

As soon as I do this, he grabs my waist and cuddles me into his arms. I am caught off guard by this.

"Here's the list of movies. Which one do you want to watch?" he asks me.

My body slightly freezes up. I assume that we are going to have sex. I feel I have no choice but to do so. Could I just walk out and give him the deuces? I'm already here and trapped in his room.

"It doesn't matter. We can watch whatever," I respond.

He stares at me and smiles. "Okay. Let's watch one of my favorites," he says, clicking play on the movie.

He takes his muscular arms and picks me up, laying me down in front of him. He wraps his arm around my stomach as the movie begins. It gets to the three-minute mark, and I feel him starting to kiss my neck. I stay still, letting him continue to kiss me. I like how it feels, but I don't know what to do next. He eventually turns me over, gets on top of me, and we begin making out.

He slides his tongue between my lips, and I follow his move. He gets up, quickly removes his shirt, and leans back over me. His six-pack is bulging, and his skin is yellow and gleaming. We continue to make out as I wrap my arms around his neck. We do this for a while. Suddenly, he moves his hands to the tie of my pants and begins pulling on the string.

We are actually about to have sex.

He gets my pants loose and wiggles them off my legs. I look up as he stands up and grabs a condom. He quickly comes back into my sight and slides his pants off of his body, then his boxers. He leans over slowly, sliding my panties off my thighs. He begins to give me kisses below, making his way up to my navel, neck, then lips. My body trembles at his kisses. I stare up at his face; his eyes look dead into mine. He lays in between my thighs and enters my body.

I immediately scream out when he enters me. I realize he is the only guy who has entered my body since my boyfriend in high school. He grips my waist tightly and bounces me on him. He finishes, then crawls under me and cuddles me tightly.

"I hope that was cool for you," he says, breathing heavily.

I turn my head sideways to see his face.

"What do you mean? Why wouldn't it be cool for me?" I ask him.

He moves from under me and lays on the other side of the bed.

"I know you're probably used to certain guys," he says.

I position myself to sit up.

"What do you mean I'm used to other guys?" I asked, confused.

"You know, black guys," he says to me.

"I'm Spanish, and I have never been with a black girl before, so I guess it's a new experience for the both of us," he tells me.

He goes to the bathroom, and I immediately search for my panties and pants.

"I guess so," I respond.

That was super awkward. I don't understand why he just made that conclusion. Does he think I'm stretched or something? Maybe he thinks I'm used to dealing with guys bigger than his size? He thinks I'm some hoe or something, but I guess if I smashed him, I would be one. I'm starting to believe I'm the hoe Stalker has told everyone about. Maybe the word spread to him, too.

"It's late, and I think I'm going to head out!" I say to him while he's still in the bathroom.

He comes out with clothes on, and I am fully dressed. I look at the clock, and it is 3:30 a.m.

"Okay," he responds.

He leads me out of the room and to the front door.

"This was nice," he tells me.

"Yeah, it was cool," I say to him.

We say our goodbyes, and I walk out the door. I pass Marcus and Stalker's building and up the steps to my apartment. With my mind racing, I run into my bathroom and immediately begin running hot water for a shower. I undress quickly, jumping into the shower and staring blankly at the faucet. What have I done? I just let a stranger into my body. I'm a hoe. I have turned into one of those girls I talk down upon. Why didn't I just leave? What's wrong with me?

Tears slowly begin to fall from my face, but my eyes remain still, and my body remains frozen. Once I leave the shower, I find my phone and call Tasha at 4:00 a.m.

Chapter Nine

THE BIG BLOW UP

The next day, I don't leave bed until 2 p.m. When I look at my phone, I see a text from the guy who texted me this morning asking me to take a Plan B pill.

"I know I used a condom, but I want to be extra safe. I'll come over and give you the pill," the message reads.

I have a text from Tasha, but I ignore it. I get out of bed and go into the kitchen to get something to eat. None of my roommates are here, and I'm enjoying every moment of being alone right now. For the first time, I don't mind being alone. The guy knocked on my door, and I opened it for him.

"Hey! How are you feeling?" he asked me.

"I'm feeling good," I lied to him. "How about you?"

He tells me he's okay and hands me the pill to take. I take it, and he begins talking with me about something unimportant. He then hugs me and tells me to call him anytime to hang out. I lie and tell him I will, and he leaves my apartment.

I close the front door and amble into my room to return to bed when my phone buzzes several times. I look down and see messages from Stalker.

"Hey, what are you doing? Meet me at my place in a couple hours to study," the messages read.

I stand entirely frozen in the hallway. I continue to stare at the messages as if they will disappear. We haven't talked or hung out in a month and some days. He and I have never studied before, so I'm confused about why he wants to now. What if he knows about what I did with the guy last night? It's perfect timing that he would hit me up as soon as the guy just left my place. Or it could be worse! What if he saw me enter the guy's apartment last night? He could have been casually stalking me and saw me coming or leaving from the guy's building. I begin to panic inside. I don't know what to expect if I go to his place. It's not like I ever did in the first place.

"Ok," I reply.

I finally move from the hallway and back into my bed. I pull the covers over me and stare blankly at the ceiling. What are we going to say to each other? Are we ever going to talk about what happened between us? There are more questions than answers available. My eyes begin to shut as I fall into a deep nap. I wake up to realize that two hours have passed, and Stalker has sent me another message.

"Are you on your way over? I left the door unlocked," his message reads.

I jump up from my bed and go directly into the bathroom. I glance at my face, and my flesh seems drained. I brush my hair upward into a messy bun, grab my backpack, and head over to Stalker's place in my pajamas.

I quickly glance at Marcus's front door before I enter Stalker's apartment. I miss our late-night talks in the study room. I slowly turn the doorknob and walk into the living room. The lights in the apartment are off, but I see the light from his room and softly knock on his door two times before I enter. His room is neat, as if he just cleaned it. He is sitting at his desk with homework in front of him and watching something sports-related on TV.

He doesn't speak to me. He nods his head at me and continues to watch the game. I jump on his bed and take my laptop out to do homework. For the first time, I don't mind us talking if he doesn't want to. For a few minutes, we just sit there with nothing but the TV's sound to keep it from being completely silent.

"Do you know how to solve this problem?" he asks me while walking over to the bed.

He carries over a paper of mathematical problems and points at the one he's inquiring about. I've always been a words girl rather than a numbers girl. I look up at him and shake my head.

"No. Why do you ask?" I asked back.

He doesn't answer my question as usual. He begins explaining how to solve the answer to the problem. He leans down near me and tells me about all the mathematical equations and rules I need to know to solve it. Once he gets the answer, he circles it multiple times with his pencil and stares at me. I stare back with the most confused look on my face.

"You didn't know how to solve this, so you're stupid," he affirms me.

I begin laughing.

"That statement doesn't even make sense! At this point, I'm not surprised by what you would say and do," I tell him.

He stares at me while he goes back to his desk. We go back to being silent.

"Why did you invite me over?" I ask, breaking the silence.

He turns his chair to face me.

"How come you don't invite me over to your place?" he responds.

"What?!" I ask.

"You always come over here. You never invited me back to your place," he explains.

I pause a moment before answering. "I mean, I never thought about it, and secondly, my roommate hates you from when you randomly DM'd her! Remember that?"

He begins smiling as he stands up from his chair and walks to the corner of the room. I follow his movements closely with my eyes.

"I could hurt your feelings If I wanted to," he says, smirking.

I stand up from my spot on his bed and stare dead at him.

"Please do," I respond.

He turns around from the corner and begins staring at me.

"You think you the only girl I talk to? I'm fucking like two other girls," he admits.

My heart sinks into my stomach. I feel my throat swell up. My eyes begin to water.

"Okay," I say.

I suck back the tears to avoid giving him the satisfaction he is seeking.

"You're just one of my hoes, like I just be playing around with you," he continues.

"How am I one of your hoes if we never had actual sex? But I know that's what you've been going around telling everybody!" I cry out.

"Remember that one night you told me we should talk more? What the fuck do you want? Seven days a week?" he says, frustrated.

"No! We only talk twice a month, so I just said we could talk more than that!" I yell.

"Well, I can't give you that!" he screams back.

He is staring angrily at me with wide eyes. I don't even know what I did to make him this upset at me.

I look at him and then look out the window before responding. "Okay. How about you fuck with who you fuck with, and I'm going to continue to fuck with who I fuck with. We don't have to do anything with each other anymore."

He quickly moves out of the corner and stands before me.

"You not fucking with no other dudes! What are you talking about? I'm the only dude you've been talking to!" he yells in my face.

"You're not the only dude I've been talking to! You think I was just waiting around for you?!" I scream back at him.

He laughs as he moves back towards the corner.

"You childish! You are like a kid who is lying, saying they fucking when they're a virgin. You not fucking with no other dudes, I know you not!" he tells me.

"Why would I lie about fucking dudes?" I scream.

"Because you didn't want me to know I was the only dude you talked to!" he says.

I look down at my phone and scroll to the messages I received from the guy this morning about taking the Plan B pill.

"If I'm lying about fucking other dudes, explain these messages to me?" I ask him as I hold up my phone for him to take a look.

He quickly glances at my phone and snatches it up in his hands. He sticks the phone as close to his eyeballs before going blind. His eyes shift swiftly back and forth as he reads each message. I follow them as I watch his face tense up. When he finishes reading, he keeps my phone in his hands. His eyes become small and watery.

"Wow. You are out here fucking," he says disappointedly.

His energy completely changes. He goes from being hyped to looking like he wants to nap. He finally releases my phone and lets it drop onto the bed. Then, he walks away from me and back to the corner of his room.

The room fills up with sadness and silence.

"Well, I have to get up early, so I think I'm going to sleep," he mumbles with a soft and low voice.

This is the first time I've seen him like this—quiet, sad, showing his insecurities.

"Okay, I'll just head out," I say in a fatigued tone.

I'm still upset and hurt by the words that came out of his mouth earlier.

"Before you go, you should know everything I said earlier was a lie. I am not fucking two other girls or anything. I'm still a virgin. I just wanted to see what you would say," he admits to me.

I look back at him with owl eyes.

"You mean to tell me you just lied about everything you said!" I scream.

"Yeah, I just made it all up," he says, getting up and walking toward the door.

I quickly gather my things from his bed. I walk briskly out of his room and apartment building without saying anything more. I don't look back at him. I keep walking until I reach my apartment door. How could he lie to me like that? He knew those lies would hurt me. This was all a joke to him. Why did he choose me to play these games with? Why did he get all sad when I showed him those text messages? Was he shocked that I would have been with someone else? The reason why I slept with that guy last night was because I couldn't sleep with him.

If only he had told me how he felt. He said he lied, but why did that girl know who I was at that event? He lied about my name. There are too many questions and not one answer. This is just too much to handle. This will be the last time I deal with him, the last time I hear another lie, and the last time I see him again.

There is one thing I took away from this night. I have feelings for him. He made me feel vulnerable. I may have fallen in love with him in some weird way, but his words hurt me too deeply. I almost cried in front of him. I almost cried out for him. He thought he would play me and not feel any pain back. I bet he learned that doesn't work. The truth is, I'm not even sure if he's as hurt as I am. He seemed like he was, but nothing can compare to the agony I feel right now.

I run back to my room and hop into my bed. At first, I feel anger, and then I feel complete sorrow. I realize I am hurt badly. I begin sobbing softly onto my pillow.

I don't want to speak to anyone anymore.

Chapter Ten:
BACK TO THE STUDY ROOM

The next few days pass, and I need someone to talk to. I would call Tasha, but she just wants to hear the gossip and does not understand my true feelings. I need some advice and clarity. I need Marcus.

After finishing my classes, I take the next shuttle bus home and sit in the back. I pull out my phone and scroll to Marcus's name in my contacts. I stare at it for a few minutes before I find the courage to send him a message.

"Hey, buddy! It's been a while, but I could chill in the study room with you," I type.

Once I send it, I slide my head onto the window and stare blankly into the trees. My mind is still racing from the big blow-up with Stalker.

A few minutes pass before I hear my phone buzz.

"Hey! You're right. It's been a minute. Let's meet in the study room now," Marcus replies.

I immediately began smiling. I knew he still had some love for me. For once in these last couple of months, I am happy. I always feel so glad when Marcus and I meet up. I know we'll talk a lot, laugh a lot, and have a lot of fun. When the shuttle arrives at the apartments, I storm off, run through the backdoor of the leasing office, and enter our study room, where Marcus is sitting with his laptop open.

"Well, Well! Look who it is!" I say excitedly.

He looks up at me and stands up with his arms out.

"What's going on, DJ!" he says to me.

I run into his arms like a child as he embraces me. I could never get tired of hugging him.

"I'm doing okay," I respond.

We release our arms and sit down across from each other. He senses the sadness in my voice.

"You don't sound like you're doing okay. Is there something bothering you?" He questions.

I stare at him in his eyes, looking into his soul. My eyes begin to water.

He immediately gets up and comes over to comfort me.

"I've been going through a lot emotionally, and you're the only person I feel I can talk to about it," I cry out.

"I'm here. I'm always here for you," he tells me softly.

"Is it Tomo?" he asks with a concerned voice.

"Yes, and someone else," I say.

He pulls his chair closer to mine and stares at me with focused eyes.

"I haven't felt like myself. I've been doing things and allowing things I never thought I would. The other night, I had a one-night stand with a guy for the first time. A little bit later, I found out he was a football player! My golden rule was never fuck a football player because they are straight hoes! I barely knew him and feel so bad inside for doing it because I didn't want to do it in the first place!" I cry out to Marcus.

His eyes are big, and his posture is tense. He opens up his arms and gives me a warm smile. I lean into him for a hug and stay there.

"It's okay. You are not a hoe or anything like that. You're the sweetest and most conscious person I know," he says to me.

I lean out of his arms and give him a warm smile.

"Don't be hard on yourself. We all do things we wish we didn't do. If anything, you learn from the situation, right?" he asks me.

I laugh and nod my head.

"You're right! I learned a lot within these past few months," I agree with him.

"Now, what did Tomo do?" he asks impatiently.

He seems as if he might explode if I mention anything too harsh. I take a deep breath and tell him about the big blow-up.

"Tomo and I had been getting intimate over the past months. Not having sex, but you know, kissing, touching, playing," I tell him.

I glance over at his face, and it doesn't look surprised.

"I was mad because we would hang out at his place at night, and he would be nice. Then, he would see me and not speak in public, and it was bothering me," I confess.

"So why did you even deal with him?" he asks in a confused tone. "You deserve someone else who can give you so much more than that!" he yells at me.

In my head, I wonder if he means someone like him, but I ignore it.

"Yes! You're right. I don't know why I continued to mess with him," I admit.

"Yeah! Especially after the fight!" I thought you told me you didn't talk to him?" he questions.

He knew I was lying but wanted me to admit my guilt.

"I lied. I didn't want you judging me about why I would talk to him after he got physical with me," I say.

He gets up from my side and walks to the other side of the table, where he had initially been sitting.

"Why did you think I would judge you? We have talked about everything in your life! I've been there for you, haven't I?" he says, frustrated.

I quickly get up and go around the table to sit next to him. "You have, and I've been so lucky to call you my best friend," I say.

He laughs.

"Of Course. Now, can I talk to you about what's been bothering me?" he says with a slight attitude.

"Yes! Please! I don't want to keep talking about myself. I'm here for you, too." I say.

Marcus begins talking about personal things in his life, and I listen to him exactly how he listens to me. Before I know it, I forget about all my problems and begin laughing and existing with Marcus. I'm glad Marcus exists. He doesn't seem that mad at me about the lie, and he talks with me about things he's never shared. We spend the next three hours talking in the study room—just like old times.

* * *

It's the end of the semester, and things have gotten a little better. Marcus and I have been hanging out on our usual schedule, and Tasha has joined us a few times.

I invited Marcus, Tasha, and Alonzo to my place for dinner and to hang out. I wanted to do something special for them because I appreciate their presence and help to get me through this tough freshman year.

I hear the doorbell ring, and I run to answer it.

"What up DJ! It smells good in here, girl!" Marcus and Alonzo yell out.

I hug them each and tell them to sit anywhere they want at the kitchen table. I set up a plate of white rice, steamed broccoli, teriyaki chicken, and dinner rolls elegantly in a row. I take out my phone to see if Tasha is on her way. When I finish the text, I see Marcus staring at my hips. I ignore it and walk back over to the table.

"Wow DJ! This is nice!" Marcus says, smiling.

"Yeah! I didn't know you could throw down like this!" Alonzo adds.

They both begin bending over the plates to smell the food.

"Hey, Hey! No touching until Tasha gets here," I tell them.

"Oh! Tasha is coming? This may end up being a perfect night!" Alonzo says, and

we all laugh out loud.

"I knew you were feeling her!" I say to him.

There is a knock on the door, and I know it's Tasha.

"Well, Well!" I say out loud as I go to answer the door.

Tasha is dressed up cute and casual and hugs me as soon as I open the door.

"Hey, girlie! You look so cute in this dress!" she screams to me.

"Hey, enough with the girl talk over there. We are trying to eat!" Alonzo yells.

I notice Alonzo has snuck a piece of chicken before I tell them to eat, so I find something to hit him with. Tasha sits next to me, and the guys stare at us from across the counter.

"I just wanted to invite you guys over and thank you for being cool and fun friends this semester. It would have been different if you weren't in my life!" I say to them.

They all look up at me with glossy eyes and agree that this semester has been fun, especially in the study rooms.

"Alright! Let's eat!" I say, extending my arms out across the food.

"This food is fire," Marcus says to me while eating.

"Thank you! But finish chewing first!" I tell him.

He looks up at me, smiles, and continues eating.

The boys are pigging out as if they haven't eaten all day.

Once we finish eating, we start talking about the semester and the goofy things we've done to each other. Alonzo stands up and begins doing that funny dance, and Marcus finds the song to play out loud on a speaker. Tasha and I are cracking up watching him do this dance for the 100th time. When he finishes, Tasha and I get up and start dancing. Alonzo and Marcus watch us from their seats. I spin Tasha around, and she turns me.

I receive a text from Myesha asking if I can print off a copy of our leasing agreements by tonight so she can turn it in to the office by tomorrow morning.

"Hey guys! I'm going to the lab super quick to print something off. I'll be right back, I promise," I say to them.

They nod, and I head out the door and into the computer room. I look down at my phone, and it's a text from Marcus.

"You look real good in that dress, by the way," he says with a smiley face emoji at the end.

I stare down at the message, confused. Is he being friendly or being flirty? Why would he send an emoji with the message? I would hate to think that the guy I call my best friend sees me more than I think. Does he like me? If he does, he's never talked about that with me. I think he mentioned something about liking another girl; there's no way he likes me. We are just friends. At least, that's what I've been thinking this entire time. I ignore the message and continue printing the papers Myesha needs from me.

I get back to the apartment, and Alonzo is goofing off in front of Tasha, and she is laughing too hard. Marcus is just sitting back. When I enter, he smiles at me and stares me down by the doorway.

"Hey guys! It's getting late, so I think we should call it a night, but we need to all hang out again before we leave for the summer," I say.

"Definitely! We can plan that! Maybe we can get frozen alcoholic drinks and chill out in the study room one last time, " Alonzo suggests.

Yeah! That's a good idea, man!" Marcus responds.

Tasha and I nod our heads as the boys get up to hug us before leaving. We say our goodbyes, and Marcus tells me he'll contact me about the hangout.

"Girl! Marcus's eyes were all over you tonight!" Tasha screams out.

"No, they weren't! We're just friends!" I argue.

"Well, how he looked at you says more than just friends. Has he ever told you he likes you?" she asks me.

I walk over to her and reach into my pocket to show her the text message he sent me earlier.

"See! I told you, he was watching your hips like a hawk when we were dancing!" she squeals.

I move to the nearest chair to sit down.

"This can't be. I've only looked at Marcus as a true friend this whole time. My feelings are tangled between the Stalker mess and the guy from the other night. I just need a friend right now, not more surprises," I tell Tasha.

She frowns and looks at me with sad eyes.

"Or maybe he's just being nice. Maybe he doesn't like you like that. You said he had never mentioned that to you before. I just know he was eyeing you," she tells me.

She leans over my chair to hug me.

"Text me about the last hangout!" she says before closing the door.

I sit in silence. If Marcus likes me, I don't know what to do. He's a great guy, and he's been here for me, but I never felt any physical attraction between us. I never examined his body more than his face and his height. I get up from my seat and walk over to the pile of dirty dishes that clutter the sink. I'm going to choose to ignore my thoughts. I don't want to think that Marcus sees me as more than I do.

"We are just friends," I whisper to myself. "We are just friends."

Chapter Eleven:
BLINDSIDED

The next day, Marcus texts me to meet him in the study room once I get home from campus. I rush off the shuttle bus and dart into the study room door, only to see Marcus sitting and talking with Stalker.

My stomach drops.

"Hey, DJ," Marcus says to me.

He gets up to hug me. I keep my eyes on Stalker as I put only one shoulder over Marcus's arm. Stalker doesn't look at me. He is staring down at a school book and writing things down on a piece of paper.

"What's going on here?" I ask Marcus as I sit my things down.

"I was just leaving," Stalker says out loud.

He gathers his things in his backpack and walks to Marcus to give him a dap.

"I'll see you later, man," Stalker says to Marcus before leaving the study room.

He doesn't look back.

CHAPTER ELEVEN: BLINDSIDED

"What are you doing hanging out with him here?" I question Marcus.

I stare over at him with a frustrated face.

"He just happened to walk by and needed help with algorithm homework," Marcus explains.

"Why didn't you tell me he was in here? I would have come by later or something," I tell him.

He quickly glances over at me, then down at his computer screen.

"I didn't think it would be a big deal," he says.

"After all I told you about us, wouldn't you think it would be a big deal?" I question.

"You guys made up after the fight, so I didn't think it was a big problem," he tells me.

I stand up and curl my face at him.

"Oh! That's your way of being funny? I don't want to be near him. Not after everything he's put me through! Also, what happened to you guys not being cool like that?" I ask.

He closes his laptop screen and stands up to face me.

"We're cordial. I won't be mad at him because of what you and he went through. You decided to deal with him that way at the end of the day," he tells me.

My body freezes up.

"So, you're saying I deserved to get treated the way I did by him, huh?" I cry out.

"No, but you did make a choice! Didn't you?" he questions.

My face falls, and I can feel my eyes begin to water.

"Wow! So, I'm the one to blame for everything and not him.

You act like he didn't do anything wrong! Some friend, you are chopping it up with an enemy!" I admit to him.

"How is he your enemy when you almost had sex with him!" he screams in my face.

I stare at him with my mouth wide open and disappointment in my eyes.

"Look, I didn't mean..." he begins to say.

I quickly swoop my backpack up to my arms and storm out of the study room.

I can't believe those words just came out of his mouth. I sprint up the stairs to my apartment and into my room and slam the door. Tears start dropping out of my eyelids.

"What did I do to deserve all of this!" I yell out to myself.

I throw myself on the ground and sink myself into the carpet. I hear my phone buzz, but I can't answer it. My heart is so heavy that it's becoming hard to carry around. My breath is becoming thinner and thinner. My eyes are starting to dry out from all the tears. All I wanted was a cool guy friend I could laugh with. I never asked for intimacy. I guess I should have known that boys can't be your friends.

After two hours of sorrow, I finally find the courage to look at my phone. It's a text from Marcus.

"DJ, I'm so sorry about earlier. I didn't mean to blame you in any way. I was trying to be an understanding friend to you and Tomo, but I was biased. I just want us to move forward and be best friends again! So, can we please plan our last hang out before the semester ends, and I won't be able to see you again?" the message reads.

I read the message about 10 times before I responded.

"I still want to be friends too. I wouldn't have told you anything about Tomo and me if I knew you two were friends. I know you'll graduate this year, and I want to hang out before you go," I respond.

I pick myself off the floor and go into the bathroom to wash my face. I stare deeply into my eyes for 10 minutes and see someone I do not recognize. My phone buzzes again.

"I'm glad you feel the same! Well, how about you meet Alonzo and me at my place? Then, we can pick up Tasha from campus, get drinks, and head back to the study room to chill. There may even be a party going on tomorrow night, too," Marcus messages me.

"That sounds cool. I'll let Tasha know."

"Cool! See you tomorrow!' Marcus texts back.

* * *

On the last day of classes before finals week, Tasha and I are sitting outside on campus with a few friends, planning a study hall to cram our brains with as much information as possible before our brains explode! Her mood seems slightly off, and she has been frowning all day.

"What's wrong, pretty girl?" I ask her.

She looks up from her textbook and into my eyes.

"I found out my boyfriend was cheating on me with a girl back home," she admits.

I look at her and frown. I put my pen down and wrap my arms around her head. She drops her head on top of my shoulder and begins to cry.

"It's going to be okay, Tasha. These dudes have been goofy out here, and they don't appreciate us, but it's cool. You deserve better and are too pretty to cry over a bum!" I say to her.

She lifts her head off my shoulder and laughs out loud. She begins smiling wide!

"Leave it up to you to make me feel better, boy!" she tells me.

"Marcus said he and Alonzo are down to hang out tonight. They said they'll pick you up from campus, buy us some drinks, and then we'll all hang out in the study room! How does that sound?" I ask her.

Her face lights up, and I can see the girl I know beginning to come out.

"Girl! Hell yes! I'm trying to see Alonzo's fine ass again! Just tell me the time!" she yells out.

I laugh as our other friends look at us, puzzled.

"So, has everything been good with you and Marcus?" Tasha questions.

"We had a little argument the other night, but we're all good for tonight," I tell her.

I know she's about to ask me about all the details.

"Arguing over what? Stalker?" she guesses.

I look over at her with wide eyes.

"How did you know it would be about Stalker?" I ask her.

"Girl! I don't know, but if he likes you, he would want to know who you were intimate with," she explains.

"It was about him. Marcus told me to meet him in the study room yesterday, and when I walked in, he was talking with Stalker." I tell her.

Her mouth drops open as if I just spilled something on my shirt.

"What! They're friends! They've been talking about you this entire time! You didn't smash Stalker, did you?" she asks me.

I gaze at her with a blank face.

"No! I did not have sex with Stalker. We got close, but it never happened! I'm unsure if Stalker has told Marcus all the details of our relationship," I say.

"Maybe he did, maybe he didn't," Tasha says as she looks back at her textbook.

I stare up into the trees and let the breeze hit my face. There's a big chance that Stalker and Marcus have been talking about me since the beginning of the school year. I can't imagine Marcus, the guy I told deep secrets, to tell Stalker everything, but after last night, maybe he could have.

"Aren't they graduating this year?" Tasha asks me, interrupting my thoughts.

"Yeah. We won't have Marcus and Alonzo to hang out with anymore. That's why we need to have fun tonight!" I say.

"Yes! We all need to get super drunk and just go all out! Let's make this a night to remember!" Tasha yells out.

"Yes! Okay, girl! Dang!" I scream back.

We both laugh and finish up our study hall for our following classes.

Once classes on campus finish, I hurry to the shuttle and jump on the bus before it pulls off. The bus driver laughs at my effort, and I roam the aisles to find a good place to sit. The bus stops again to let a last-minute passenger on, and it's Stalker. He quickly jumps on the bus, walks past the aisles, and chooses to sit two seats in front of me. Before he sits, he gives me a quick look and turns away.

I want to get up and talk to him, but I can't. When I see him, my voice fades, and my body freezes. I feel like he is mad at me for something. Could it be the text messages I showed him from the big blowup? I just feel guilty when I stare at him. I wish we could have a normal adult conversation about everything that happened between us.

When the shuttle bus stops, Stalker springs out of his seat and heads for the door. I follow directly behind him, tracing his every move. As soon as he gets off the bus, he begins power-walking toward his building. He turns to the side, glances at me, and continues walking. He knows that I'm following him.

"Tomo!" I yell.

He continues to walk ahead.

"Tomo!" I yell out louder.

He picks up his speed and darts up the stairs to his building.

"I know he heard me calling him," I whisper.

I look to the right and see a person approaching me. When they get close enough, I realize that it's Marcus.

"Hey, DJ! Are you good for tonight? Alonzo and I were thinking around 8 p.m.," he tells me.

"Yeah! That sounds good. So, should I tell Tasha around 8:30 p.m.?" I ask.

"Yes! I'm so excited!" Marcus shouts out.

I laugh as I watch his smile spread across his face.

"Why are you so excited? It's not like we haven't all hung out before!" I say.

He grabs my arms and spins me around until I feel a little dizzy. I laugh and hit him to let me go.

"Because it's the last time I'll see you before the summer! Of course, we can always meet when the time is right," he tells me, looking into my eyes.

"Yeah, it's bittersweet. But you're my best friend, so we'll hang out again!" I tell him.

His face turns straight.

"That's right. We are. I'll see you at my place tonight," he says to me.

He glances at me one last time before heading up the steps Stalker used to run away from me.

What did he mean by meet up when the time is right? Ever since the flirty text the other night, I'm beginning to question everything he says to me. I walk up the steps to my apartment building and enter to find Myesha crying on the couch with a friend consoling her.

"Hey, girl. Is everything okay?" I say, rushing to her side on the couch.

"Girl, her crazy boyfriend is mad that she went to the club last night without his permission, so he's been sending her pictures of pills, saying he was about to kill himself because of her!" her friend explains to me.

My face drops as if I'm on a roller coaster.

"Are you serious!" I say in shock.

"Yes. It's true," Myesha chimes in.

Her eyes flushed with tears. She picked up her phone and began flipping through the pictures. There are pictures of pills, him with a rope around his neck, and a video of him calling her out of her name.

"I'm so sorry, love! These dudes are so fucked up! You're too amazing of a girl to deal with this!" I say to her.

I extend my arms out, and she embraces them. We sit here like this for a few minutes before I let her go. She spills out all her emotions on my plate, and I do the same to hers. It seems I haven't been the only dramatic guy on this campus.

By the time Myesha, her friend, and I finish talking about our emotions and how guys aren't shit, I go to my room to prepare to hang out with some. I remember Marcus mentioning that we might go to a party, so I dressed up slightly more than I would if it was a typical study room hang-out. I could use a party and some alcohol right now with everything that has been going on.

As I head out the door, I tell Myesha and her friend bye. They are waiting for the cops to come to the apartment to clear up the situation. I go up the stairs to Marcus's building and knock on the door. I can't help but stare at Stalker's door next to it. I wish I could just get over him.

"Hey, DJ!" Marcus says, opening the door.

He leans into me for a hug and motions for me to enter the living room. Alonzo waves at me with a big smile on the couch. They both look casual in fancy button-up tops.

"You look nice!" Marcus says, smiling. He then looks at Alonzo, who nods in approval of my outfit.

"Thanks! You mentioned we may go to a party, so I came prepared," I say.

"Yeah, we might. Y'all ready to go so we can pick up Tasha?" Alonzo says impatiently.

I look over at him and down at my phone to text Tasha, saying we're on the way.

"Sure! Let's go!" I scream.

They laugh as we head out of the building and down to Alonzo's car. Marcus and I begin talking as if we're just in the study room with us two. Once we reach the first stoplight, I notice Alonzo has turned wrong toward Tasha's dorm.

"Hey, Alonzo, campus is back that way," I inform him.

He looks at me from the side and nods his head.

"I know. I just need to stop by my place real quick to get something.

"Okay," I say in a weird voice.

I look over at Marcus, and he and Alonzo are whispering to each other. We pull up at Alonzo's house, and he welcomes Marcus and me inside while he gets what he needs. I look around, astonished because I've never stepped foot in Alonzo's place this year. It's clean, fully furnished, and retro. Alonzo reaches into his closet and changes his shoes. Then, he finds a different shirt and switches it out with his current one.

I look at his actions, puzzled. Why is he changing his shirt and shoes as if something was wrong with what we had on? He may be trying to get fresh for the party that might be happening. Marcus comes up to me and taps me on the shoulder.

"Tonight is going to be so fun! After we get Tasha, we'll go to get the liquor," he tells me.

I glance back over at Alonzo's movements before responding.

"Okay. Sounds good," I tell him.

Once Alonzo finishes playing dress-up, we return to his car and head to campus for Tasha. He bumps loud rap music, and I sing every word from the stereo. Marcus laughs at me, but Alonzo encourages me to keep going. We pull outside Tasha's dorm; she is dolled up and ready to party.

"Hey guys! What's up! It sounds like y'all already getting lit in here!" she screams to us as she opens the car door.

I lean in to hug her, and then Alonzo blasts off.

"We're just getting started!" Alonzo says.

He looks back at Tasha and gives her a wide smile. She laughs and hits me on my shoulder.

"Girl, I think he wants it!" she whispers to me in the back seat.

Alonzo stops at the nearest corner store to buy liquor. He and Marcus ask us what we want, and we start rambling many things as if we were drunk. They hear our list and nod together before getting out of the car and slamming the door like twins.

"So are we going to the party or what!?" Tasha asks excitedly.

"I'm not sure. They didn't say where the party is or whose party it even is," I tell her.

"I don't know, but Alonzo is definitely on me! You know my boyfriend and I just broke up!" she screams while giggling at herself.

I laugh back and hit her on her shoulder.

"Look! If we're not going to the party, we're going back to the study room just to chill and drink. So you need to calm all of that horny down!" I say to her.

We both start giggling when Marcus and Alonzo enter the car. They look back at us and hand us our liquor.

"What y'all two back here giggling about?" Marcus asks.

"Nothing! We're just ready to turn up!" Tasha squeals.

They laugh and give us goofy stares.

"Well, that's what we are about to do!" Alonzo tells us, putting the car in reverse and driving into the night.

Tasha and I begin downing our alcohol. We don't even take mini breaks in between. We start talking, drinking, rambling, and drinking so much more. This alcohol is strong. By the time Alonzo reaches the stop light by the apartments, I am feeling tipsy, and my words begin to slur.

Suddenly, Alonzo makes a left instead of a right where the apartment buildings sit. I get a funny feeling in my stomach and scrunch my face in confusion. I look over at Tasha, who appears to be in the same condition as me. She stares back at me, smiles, then continues to bob her head to the music.

I lean forward to the passenger seat at Marcus, who is laughing and talking with Alonzo while the stereo blasts.

"Hey, Marcus. I thought we were going back to the apartments to chill in the study room?" I ask.

Alonzo looks at Marcus, who looks over at me.

"Yeah, we decided since we have alcohol and stuff, we might just chill at Alonzo's place for a little while," he tells me.

"Oh, okay," I say. I sit back in silence, watching the streets we turn on.

Why didn't he just tell me this in the first place? I told him to tell me all the details of the night. Why did Alonzo change his shirt and shoes if we were going back over to his place anyway? How is it that he and Alonzo are forcing us to chill somewhere, and they didn't even get clearance from Tasha and me? I'm a bit upset and tipsy, but I trust these guys. I've been hanging out with them all year, and they never gave me any reason to doubt their actions.

We pull up to Alonzo's place, and our steps are sloppy.

"Y'all good? Y'all already got drunk on the way here?" Marcus says to Tasha and I.

Tasha laughs her soul out. I giggle a little and walk into Alonzo's place. Alonzo leads the way, and Marcus follows him. Tasha, next, then there's me. He leads us into his room and shuts the door behind me.

"We can just chill out here for now," he tells us.

I look around the room and feel like we've been trapped. The room is dark, lit only by a small desk light. A part of me starts to panic, but the alcohol in my system causes me to ignore this panic. Maybe I'm thinking too much of the situation and need to loosen up.

"I want to show y'all something cool!" Alonzo says.

He walks over to his colossal nightstand and turns on a big lava lamp that lights up purple.

"What! That's cool!" Tasha screams out.

She walks over to the lamp and rubs it up and down. I walk near her and just stare at it.

"This too!" he screams as he reaches for a mini remote control.

He pushes a few buttons on the remote, and his king-size mattress begins moving up and down, side to side. Tasha and I's mouths drop wide open. In all my years of living, I've never seen a bed with the same features as a massage chair at the nail shop.

"Where did you even get a bed like this!?" I yell out. " I ain't never met one dude in the hood who got a bed like this!"

He looks at me with wide eyes and laughs.

"I'm not those dudes in the hood. Welcome!" he tells me.

Tasha immediately jumps on the bed as Alonzo begins controlling it. She laughs hard, and Alonzo jumps on the bed near her. They start flirting in each other's faces. Now, I feel awkward. Marcus exits the bathroom and stands by me, watching Alonzo and Tasha flirt. I look over at him, and then he looks over at me.

"You want to join them?" he says.

"What?" I say back.

"Do you want to get on the bed and just chill? It's a little awkward standing here just watching them," he tells me.

I look back over at them, then at Marcus.

"Yeah, you're right, I guess," I say.

He smiles and motions me toward the bed. He grabs the TV remote and turns it on to drown out Tasha's and Alonzo's conversation. I sit on the edge of the bed, sipping slowly on my drink while Marcus begins sipping on his. We talk about life as if we're back in the study room. He is smiling at everything that comes out of my mouth.

Suddenly, Tasha grabs my shoulders from behind and pulls me into the bed. Alonzo jumps into Marcus and begins pushing buttons on the bed remote. We all slide up and down the bed, hitting each other. Everyone is laughing, but I can feel Marcus' hands grip my hips and thighs as I continue to slide with the group. I feel alarmed and want to stop, but the group is having so much fun.

Once we stop, Tasha and Alonzo begin cuddling up on the right side of the bed. They are touching and playing with each other intimately. Marcus and I take the left side of the bed. We are lying on our sides, facing each other.

"I knew they liked each other," Marcus says to me. He looks behind his shoulder at their side of the bed and laughs.

"Yeah, I could've figured it out," I say awkwardly.

I turn and begin watching TV to avoid looking into Marcus' eyes. My body starts to freeze up. I feel uncomfortable being this close to him in an intimate way. I'm uncomfortable with Marcus and Alonzo's plan to have us come back here. I was uncomfortable by the way Marcus was sneakily touching my body. I'm uncomfortable with Alonzo and Tasha's intimacy in front of us. I'm uncomfortable all over, but I don't say I am.

From my side view, I see Marcus watching me and sexually staring down at my thighs. I've never seen him look at me like this before. I feel a lump in my throat but keep looking forward to the screen.

"You know this show?" he asks me, trying to make small talk.

"Yeah. I think I've watched it a couple of times before," I say back without looking at him.

I pause in between words to keep my voice from cracking.

I begin explaining the show in more detail to avoid any sexual gestures that Marcus could be thinking about. He scoots down closer to me to look at me in my eyes. I lean forward to sit up instead of lying down. I continue talking. He remains in his position and begins looking up into my face. Suddenly, I can feel his hands softly rubbing my leg.

"It's getting late, and I have somewhere to go in the morning. I'm going to try to get some sleep," I say abruptly.

I quickly throw myself underneath the covers and away from Marcus's hands. I scrunch my body together and clench my teeth toward the wall. I squeeze my eyes shut as tight as I can.

"That's cool. I'm feeling kind of tired, too," he says back.

His voice fades. I feel him move closer to me before he goes quiet. There is no way I can move out of this position. There is no way I can get home from here! I don't want to be here anymore! I don't want to have sex with Marcus! I don't want to be around any guys! I don't want to have guy friends anymore! I feel a tear roll down my cheek. I want to cry out for help, but no one can save me. After 3 hours, I hear Alonzo and Tasha's voices die down. Someone has turned off the TV. There is nothing but silence.

I decide to turn around to check out the scene. I slowly turn my body from the wall and notice the time. It is 3:30 a.m. Marcus' hands are gently attached to my waist. I hadn't even known they had been there. I wiggle them off me, and Marcus opens his eyes. Instantly, I play as if I'm asleep and close my eyes quickly. I keep them squinted so I can see what he is doing. He looks at me and smiles. He takes his hands and begins rubbing my back and my shoulder. He scoots closer to mine and slides his hands back on my waist. He takes a deep breath. I continue to watch his movements. Is he going to touch me while I'm asleep?

Fifteen minutes go by, and he hasn't moved. I take this moment to try and wiggle his hands off my body. This wakes him back up. I play like I'm asleep again. This time, he leans into me and brings his face close to mine. He pokes his lips out and carries them slowly to my lips. I panic inside. Help! I don't want to kiss him. Help! I don't want sex. Help! Immediately, I fake a big yawn and swiftly turn my body to the wall again. This startles him. He removes his hands from my waist and keeps them off. I curl my body up again. I stare out the window for the rest of the night, watching the moon turn into the sun.

Chapter Twelve:
LAST HANGOUT

It's the next day, and I have not fallen asleep. I hear Tasha and Alonzo waking up, and someone goes to the bathroom. I peep over my shoulder, and Marcus is still sleeping. I quickly throw the covers off me and walk outside on the back porch for fresh air and sunlight. I don't know how this day will go, but I want to go home now.

I hear the porch door open, and a hand touches my shoulder.

"Good morning, girl! Last night was crazy," Tasha tells me. Her hair is messy, and her bra strap is down.

"Yeah, easy for you to say. You like Alonzo, and Alonzo likes you," I tell her.

She looks at me with an uneasy face and then whispers, "Did Marcus try anything last night?"

I lean into her face so the guys won't be able to hear our conversation. "He was rubbing on my thighs, and then he tried to kiss me!" I whisper back.

Tasha jumps back with her mouth dropped.

Before she can respond, Alonzo opens the porch door and motions for us to come inside.

"Hey, y'all want to chill before we drop you guys home?"

Tasha's face lights up and gets red. "Yes! Don't mind if I do!" she tells him, giggling and strutting her way back inside.

Alonzo looks at me for my answer next.

"I'll be there in a moment, just getting some air," I tell him.

He smiles slightly, then closes the door behind him.

I look out at the trees and expose my face to the sunlight. I look at the street and think about just walking home right now. I don't know how far it is, but I could figure it out. I'm unsure if I can look into Marcus' face after last night. I am entirely done with hanging out with everyone. I take a deep breath and walk back into the house.

When I go into Alonzo's room, Tasha sits on his lap with his arms around her. They are flirting and touching while the TV is on some random channel. Marcus is sitting on the edge of the other side of the bed with his eyes glued to the TV. I don't know where I should go. I don't want to be near Tasha and Alonzo, but I don't want to go near Marcus. To make things not awkward, I go over to where Marcus is sitting and grab my shoes to put on.

"Hey, Good morning," Marcus says with a smile.

"Hey," I say.

He watches me as I begin putting on my shoes.

"We're probably not leaving right now. Alonzo looks busy," he says, looking over in his direction.

"Yeah. I guess so. I promised my other friend to go to this thing with her, and I need to leave soon," I lie to him.

He looks at me straight and then back at the TV screen. We

sit silently for the next fifteen minutes, and Marcus and I can only hear Tasha, Alonzo, and the TV.

"The thing you're going to, is it an event?" Marcus breaks the silence between us.

I begin telling him more about the made-up event. He then starts talking to me about his graduation in a few days. Two hours pass, and we are still at Alonzo's place.

"Hey Alonzo, can we leave soon? I have this thing to go to, and I'm already late," I say irritatedly.

He looks up from Tasha's face.

"Um, yeah, we can go now," he says.

Everyone is staring at me with a straight face. They can feel my energy.

We all get up to go outside, and I am the first to go out the door and into the car. I ask Alonzo if he can drop me off first. The car ride home is awkward and quiet. Maybe Alonzo and Tasha saw what happened and aren't saying anything. I know for a fact that Marcus knows I curved him last night. The more I think about last night, the more I believe that Alonzo and Marcus were trying to set Tasha and me up for something we didn't consent to. That's the only reason that could explain last night.

"Alright, home at last. Have fun doing your thing," Alonzo says, pulling up in front of the leasing office.

I get out of the car and open the door.

"Yeah, girl! Have fun, and I'll see you later," Tasha tells me.

Marcus doesn't face me. He only looks at me from his peripheral vision.

"Alright, DJ. See ya," he says quietly.

I nod my head, then turn around as fast as I can. I feel in my gut that this is the last time Marcus and I would hang out. I will never see him again when I walk away from the car. At this point, I'm okay with that.

* * *

It's graduation season, and it's time to leave this town! This year has been eye-opening for me, but it's one I would rather keep in the past. Marcus and Alonzo haven't contacted me since they dropped me off that day, and I haven't contacted them. I have accepted the fact that I lost both Marcus and Stalker. Tasha and I aren't speaking as much after I found out she invited Marcus and Alonzo to eat with her at the dining halls and didn't invite me. Her excuse was she knew I was mad at them and didn't want to make me uncomfortable. She should be angry as well! They set both of us up that night, not just me!

I'm in my room, packing all my things to return home. The apartment's new manager raised the rent price for the next school year, and Myesha and I decided we would find somewhere else cheaper. I need a change of scenery anyway. I unzip my big suitcase and start throwing everything inside. My mom texts me, saying she'll be in town to pick me up in two hours. Fuck, I just got started. I grab my speaker and play some fast-tempo music to get me moving quickly.

The two hours pass, but my mom is late as usual, so I have enough time to do extra cleaning before she arrives. When she arrives, she seems tired.

"Hey, Mom!" You sure you don't want to lay down before we head back into town?" I ask her with my arms extended.

She embraces me lightly, then ambles over to the couch to sit down.

"No, I'm fine. I just need a couple of minutes. Did you clean out everything?" she questions me.

I take a seat next to her.

"Yeah, I made sure everything was the same as when I moved in so that they won't charge me any fees," I tell her.

"Good, because you know they will. How was your semester overall?" she asks.

My eyes grow big as I stare at her. My mom and I don't talk about anything personal in my life, not to mention issues with boys. Her only advice growing up was, "Don't get pregnant."

"It's been cool. A lot has happened, but I'm ready to go," I tell her.

My mom doesn't respond. She lies back on the couch and begins to nap. I turn on the TV to drown out her snoring. Once she awakes, we carry my belongings to the car and set the GPS to return to the city.

* * *

Summer is in full swing, and I'm back working 40 hours a week at the restaurant. I still take the bus back and forth, and the same employees and some new high school kids still work there. A couple of them flirt with me every shift, but I don't pay attention.

On my birthday, I get a call from Marcus. My body freezes as I look down at the call screen for what seems like five minutes. I immediately think about that night and the rumors I heard claiming Marcus was upset at me. Upset at me? What did I ever do to him? I'm the one who almost got date rape, and he's mad at me? I swipe to decline the call. I don't think I ever want to talk to him again.

The summer continues to go the same way as any typical summer in high school, except my heart is broken badly. I notice that I feel sad when I'm alone. I tend to think of Marcus and Stalker, and my mind fills up with haunting memories. One night, I cried about it all. On most days, it's all I think about.

On the plus side, Tasha and I decide to meet to resolve our issues.

"Look! I didn't invite you to the dining hall after that night because you told me you didn't want to see them anymore," Tasha tells me.

"You thought that was okay! Tasha, they lowkey tried to rape us on some sneaky type shit, and you think that's okay!" I yell at her.

"I didn't feel that way. Alonzo and I have been vibing the whole semester, so I don't think what you felt applies to me!" she says back.

"Wow! So fuck the girl code, huh? You wouldn't have met Alonzo or anybody if it weren't for me!" I remind her.

Her face gets red while she curls her face at me.

"What do you mean by that?" she asks.

"I'm just saying you lived in the dorms and knew fewer people than I did. Every chance you get, you hang around with my friends. Name one person I met from you?" I say to her.

She looks over at the bar, then back at me.

"Let's not go there. I didn't use you for no friends. You're out of line!" she responds.

I agree that I went too far, and we decide to move on from the subject. Even though we talked about what happened, Tasha may be too naive for me to be close friends with her again. Not only did they try to set us up, but she invited them out for dinner several times after! I think I'm going to keep my distance for now.

Sophomore year is approaching, and I must find a place to stay. Myesha has found another group of girls to stay with for her junior year, so I'm out of luck. The only other person I know is Tasha, and if we become roommates, I would find it impossible to keep my distance from her.

* * *

The summer ends quickly, and the first week of Sophomore year has come. The campus is booming with returning students and fresh faces. I ended up messaging another friend I got to know on a close level from freshman year. We live in a two-bedroom, two-bathroom apartment 15 minutes away from campus. This will save the long wait for the bus back and forth.

"Hey, girl!" my new roommate says to me, opening her arms wide.

I scoop her up into my arms and hug her tightly.

"What's up love! Are you excited about this semester?" I ask excitedly.

"Yes! We're roomies, and some fine new men are on this campus!" she says with a big smile on her face.

I roll my eyes at her statement.

"Come on, this semester, guys are going to be better than those guys you dealt with last year," she tells me.

"Honestly, I'm completely turned off by dudes right now. Maybe I need to find a group of bad bitches," I say back.

She laughs and begins snorting. Her snorting makes me laugh.

"Girl! You are too much! A welcome back party is happening tonight, so you need to get dressed so we can go!" she tells me.

She slaps me on the butt and leaves the apartment.

"Huh, I guess I'll go," I whisper to myself as I look into my closet for something cute to wear.

As I begin getting ready for the party, I can only think about Stalker. Over the summer, he replied to some of my social stories, and I responded with a few words. I hate to say it, but I'm craving him right now. I miss his touch, his hands massaging my thighs, his lips, his smile, his deep voice, and those big brown eyes looking into me. Maybe Stalker will be at the party, dancing on another girl like last time.

My roommate comes back with her car pulled outside, and I grab my clutch and rush out the door. After freshman year, we learned that upperclassmen arrive at parties two hours before it's over and pre-game before they get there so they can already be drunk and in the mood. I haven't had a drink, but I feel drunk off wanting intimacy. We find a decent parking spot and head in line for the security check. Let's just say I've been to several parties, and not one guard has yet confiscated my pink pepper spray.

We get into the party and head straight for the bar. My roommate, a little older than I, orders me two drinks, and I gulp them in a matter of minutes. I start seeing the room spin. My senses are heightened, and I search the crowd for Stalker.

"You want to dance?" my roommate asks me.

I look into her face, and she seems to have the same face as me. I know we are on the same page.

"Yes! Let's turn up!" I scream at her over the music.

I take her hand and guide her onto the dancefloor, and we begin dancing. This feels like old times, except this me is different. I sway my hips and put my hands up in the air as the base of the music enters my chest. My mind starts flashing memories of Stalker and me in his bedroom. They feel so real, like I'm living in the past. I lick my lips at the thought of his lips pressing against mine. I want him to caress me, hold me, fuck me, love me, all of the above. My craving for him is bigger than anything I have ever known.

My phone buzzes in my clutch, and I stop dancing to check what it is. I look down at the screen. Stalker's name pops up.

"Hey, what's up? Are you at that party? I'm not at that party, I'm at home. You should see me after. I want to see you," the message reads.

I stand stiff and silent, rereading over each message. How did he know I was thinking about him? It's like he knows how to read my mind. Could he feel my energy? Was it that strong? He and I have such a powerful but weird chemistry. It's like I've known him before, or more like he knew me before we met at the bus stop.

After pondering for a few seconds, I tell him I'll come through. A big smile appears on my face. I finally get to indulge myself with him. We haven't seen each other in a long time, and I'm unsure what to say first. I start bouncing my body to the beat of the song playing. I find my roommate dancing on a guy, and like a good sportsman, I cheer her on until her knees get tired. We go on all night until the deejay spins the last song on his playlist.

I look at my roommate and give her a look to see if she's still okay with driving.

"Yes! Girl, I'm good. We had those few drinks when we got here," she says.

She throws her hand around my neck and hugs me with a smirk.

"Can you do me a favor?" I ask with a big smile stretching across each cheek.

She shrugs at me and swings her hand down to her hip.

"What is it?" she questions.

"Can you drop me off at a guy's place tonight?" I ask.

"What! You are trying to get some action tonight! From who?" she asks, looking up at me like I'm a surprise.

"It's this guy I used to talk to. Anyway, we're not going to do anything but chill," I say.

"Girl, it's almost 1:30 a.m. Y'all smashing. I'll do it, but tell me you're safe," she says.

I smile and give her a big hug. I like how she doesn't question me about who the guy is and supports me potentially getting some long-overdue sex. We walk to the parking lot and drive off into the streets. The thought of seeing his face makes me nervous. Once we get closer to the apartments I lived in last year, I call him to see if he's in the same building.

"Hello," he says in an intense voice.

I smile instantly.

His voice is more profound than usual, and I realize this is the first time we've ever talked on the phone with each other.

"It's me. Why does your voice sound like that?" I ask him.

"What do you mean? My voice always sounds like this," he says.

"No, it doesn't. It's deeper than usual," I tell him.

"You on your way?" he asks me.

"Yes. Do you live in the same building?" I question.

He goes silent for a moment.

"No, I switched buildings. I live in the one next to my old building on the left. I'll text you my apartment number and leave the door open," he says as he hangs up the phone.

I smile inside when he says he'll leave the door open. It brings back too many memories to count. My roommate arrives in front of the leasing office, and I hop out and pull down my dress.

"Be safe, baby, and call me if you need me to come get you," she tells me.

"I will," I say.

I kiss my hand and blow it at her. She catches the kiss and places it on her chest before she drives off. It makes me laugh every time she does that.

I stroll towards Stalker's new building. What are we going to say to each other? What are we going to do? We haven't talked about anything, and I have much to get off my chest. Does he feel the same way I feel about him right now? I march up the steps and turn to face his apartment door. I look over the balcony into the streets, and everything is quiet. I guess the world is waiting to see how this night will end. I take a deep breath before opening the door and entering his room.

The look of his new apartment is different from his last one. His decor is different, but everything is tidy. He's always been clean. I look over, and he is lounging on his bed, watching TV. His eyes are low, and his skin is slightly red. I know he has been smoking weed. He turns his head to look at me and begins smiling.

"Hey. What's up?" he says, turning his head back toward the TV. He talks to me as if we just hung out yesterday.

"Nothing much. Just trying to figure out why you hit me up," I say, taking a seat in his desk chair.

We sit silently for a few minutes, staring at the TV screen. I'm getting impatient already. I'm still a little drunk, and I need him to answer all of my questions this time.

"Are you going to tell me or what?" I finally ask.

"Why is that important? What will you ask me next? What do I want from you?" he tells me.

I get up and jump on the edge of the bed to stare him in his eyes.

"Yes! I won't keep playing games with you, going back and forth. One day, I'm just not going to respond to you," I warn him.

He chuckles and gets up from the bed. He grabs my hands and pulls me up into his arms. He gently rocks my body back and forth in his grip slowly.

"You look fine as hell right now. I miss you, okay?" he says, smiling wide and staring into my soul.

His eyes are so low I can barely see them, but I know they focus only on me. I smile back at him.

"I miss you too," I admit softly.

"You need to take this dress off," he says, tugging on the dress around my waist.

I look up at him in shock. He must finally want me as bad as I want him.

"Dang! Are you trying to get me naked right now?" I ask.

He goes into his drawer and hands me a pair of grey sweatpants.

"Here, put these on," he demands of me.

His eyes follow every moment I make, waiting for me to reveal my body to him. I look deeply into his eyes before I slide the pants up my legs, then take off the dress like a t-shirt. I am now in my bra and my brand-new pants. He stares down at my body, then jumps back onto the bed and puts his hands behind his head. He doesn't say anything. He just smiles with his eyes squinted as if he needs glasses.

The room goes silent. I take my body and climb on top of his. I roll my head onto his chest. I can feel every bone and muscle in his body. I look up at his face, and it hasn't changed. Time feels like it has stopped moving. I can hear and feel my heartbeat pumping loudly outside my chest. I begin counting how many times I listen to it beat. After counting a couple of times, I hear a heartbeat that does not belong to me. I push my ear into his chest and feel his heartbeat thumping against it. I follow his rhythm, then mine, his, and realize our hearts are pumping to the same rhythm.

I continue to listen to the rhythm of our heartbeats. I feel a deep connection with him that I can't even explain. Suddenly, I feel two arms slowly run down my back. When I look up, he is staring right at me. I stare into his eyes and instantly become hypnotized. He leans into me and sticks his tongue between my lips, and we begin making out. We twist, we turn, we soar. He lifts me by my arms and swings me onto his lap. My entire body becomes hypersensitive to his touch. It's as if some natural drug is taking over my body, but what could it be?

He begins feeling my body in all the right places. I start rubbing him down for his good behavior. Our bodies intertwine with each other like tied shoelaces. I aggressively grab onto his zipper and pull on it. I want him now. He follows my hand, digs his hand into his pants, and pulls out flesh that's long and hard. I look down at it, then stare up at him. I take my hand and begin massaging it up and down fast. His mouth opens wide as he grips the side of my thighs tightly. He doesn't go for my pants or touch my ever-flowing river. After a few minutes, he finishes, and we both sink onto the bed, hugging each other's bodies.

I throw my head on his chest as he caresses my shoulder. I feel embarrassed. I feel like an idiot for wanting to have sex with him and him not wanting to have sex with me after all this time. He hasn't even tried to touch what's between me. This was supposed to be the night. I waited for him all last year, and he still doesn't want me. I know things will never change between him and me, no matter how long I stay around and wait. We lie cuddled with each other for a while before I reach for my phone and check the time.

"It's getting late. I think I should get out of here," I tell him as I lift my head from his chest.

He follows my every move.

"Okay. You need me to call your friend back to come get you?" he asks me.

I look over at him with a puzzled face.

"Why would I need you to do that? I can just call her myself," I tell him.

He laughs and reaches to rub my back.

"It's pretty late. So, if she says no, I can persuade her with my charming voice," he says to me.

I smirk and remove myself from the bed to adjust my clothes.

"I'm good. I'll just call a ride," I tell him.

He gets off the bed, walks behind me, and softly kisses my neck.

"Let me call for you," he says into my ear.

He grabs his phone, presses a few buttons, and claims the ride is three minutes away.

"Cool," I say back.

I go into the corner and find my shoes upside down. He watches me as I put them on and notices my mood has changed.

"What's up? You good?" he asks me.

"Yeah, I'm good. I'm just tired," I say softly to him.

I try hard to fight back against the words I want to say: You played me. I thought you cared about me, and I thought you wanted me.

I get up and head out of his room to the front door. He follows closely behind me. When the driver arrives, his phone buzzes, and he looks at me and nods. I open the door and proceed to walk out.

"Hey!" he screams, grabbing onto my arm.

I turn to look back at him.

"If you ever want to come over or anything, don't hesitate to hit me up, like any time you want," he tells me with those big brown eyes.

"I will," I lie with a fake smile.

He releases my arm, and I walk ahead without looking back.

This will be the last time we see, touch, or kiss each other again. A tear rolls down my face as I get into the car. The love I have for him is toxic. After all, he abused me. A person who loves me wouldn't do that. If this is love, then I deserve better than love. I can't continue to allow myself to be hurt by the same guy. I look out the window at my old apartment complex and remember all the memories made here.

I came to college, desperately trying to escape my life back home, but it seems to have followed me. I finally realize that boys are my issue. This whole year, I gave them all my energy and my time. My grades fell behind, and I didn't even explore myself and my interests outside of them. I want to see the good in them, even when there is none. Forget about them. I need to bring out the good in myself, focus on myself, and love myself. I smile at the thought of this.

"Had a good night?" the driver asks me.

"Yeah, this has been the best night I've had in a while," I say to him.

www.ingramcontent.com/pod-product-compliance
Lightning Source LLC
Chambersburg PA
CBHW050452110726
47899CB00003B/915